THE LEGEND OF
BROKEN SADDLE

The Legend of Broken Saddle

WILL BLACK

A Black Horse Western

ROBERT HALE · LONDON

ISBN 0 7090 5976 0

Robert Hale Limited
Clerkenwell House
Clerkenwell Green
London EC1R 0HT

Photoset in North Wales by
Derek Doyle & Associates, Mold, Clwyd.
Printed and bound in Great Britain by
WBC Ltd, Bridgend, Mid-Glamorgan.

To Mikki and Ron and their new sheep shed
— and for pulling me out of the snow!

ONE

The sky was a deep blood-red as the lone wagon painfully made its way westwards, heading, it seemed, straight towards the dull yellow disc that even as the men watched, began to dip behind the the mountains of the Sierra Nevada.

The wagon was overloaded. Originally, there had been three, but terrain and badmen had seen to it that this was the sole survivor of a journey of nearly four-thousand miles that had started out of Boston five months before.

The three families had been lucky. But then, luck was as you found it. Six dead, two wagons lost. Luck? The survivors thought so.

The trouble had started when they were less than two weeks out of Boston.

The lead wagon carrying the family Dowie, Ben, his wife Martha and two boys, Billy and Joe, broke a rear axle. The repairs took two days to carry out and in that time, one of the boys, Billy, out playing on his own, was bitten by a rattle-snake.

It took Billy six hours to die.

The Dowie family would have liked more time to mourn the death of their son, but the New Land wouldn't allow that.

No sooner had they buried him in a shady spot under one of the few cottonwoods around, than they were attacked by a gang of bandits.

With only three wagons, they could hardly form a circle and protect themselves from all sides, but they did their best.

Their four attackers rode round and round the wagons, taking pot-shots from the saddle. At first, things went the settlers' way; one of the bandits was hit and he slumped forward in his saddle, taking no further part in the action.

The three familes hid the women and children behind them as the men continued the fight. Along with Ben Dowie fought Doug Cartwright, Patrick, Seamus and Thadius Malloy, son, father and uncle, respectively.

The Malloys were no shootists; they'd thought that the journey out from Ireland had been the hard part. They'd all survived the long sea trip, but nothing had prepared them for this.

Huddled behind the men came Siobhan, wife of Patrick, Pat junior and Eileen, their children, and Margaret, their grandmother. Next to them Martha and Joe Dowie, Joe protecting Eileen whom he'd taken a shine to.

Completing the settlers was Beth-Ann, newly married to Doug and Ben Dowie's father, Bertram.

All in all thirteen souls who thought they only

had the elements to contend with, but now found themselves under attack.

The remaining desperadoes leapt from their saddles and split up. Leaving their wounded companion to take care of the animals, they began their attack in earnest.

The three men knew how to use their weapons and, although outnumbered, had that advantage. Most of the shots from the wagons thudded harmlessly into the ground, or flew equally ineffectually through the air.

The badmen had acted out this scenario many times before. Settlers were easy pickings and, if you waited just a couple of weeks after they set off, it didn't usually take long to hi-jack them and steal their possessions. Getting the stuff back to Boston and sold on was easy, especially when so many other settlers were stocking up for the long trip out West.

The three men took their time and made each shot count.

Seamus Malloy was the first to be hit. He caught a slug in the forehead and didn't utter a sound. It took Patrick a few moments to realize that his father had stopped shooting.

Margaret, his wife, crawled towards her dead husband, intent on grabbing his rifle, but she didn't stand a chance.

Before Patrick could stop her, she was up on all fours, making her way to the front of the wagon. The only thought in her head was to kill the men who'd killed her husband. She could mourn him later when all this was over, she thought.

The slug entered her chest and pierced her grieving heart before she had even picked up the discarded rifle.

Patrick Malloy froze.

In the space of two minutes, he'd watched as his mother and father were killed and there wasn't a damn thing he could do about it. For the first time, he realized he was fighting, not only for his life, but for that of his family.

The shooting continued unabated, it seemed there was nothing they could do to stop it.

Doug Cartwight took a shot high up on his shoulder and all but screamed, the pain being so intense and Beth-Ann lost no time in coming to his aid. Patrick yelled at her to stay where she was. It was if as he was watching his mother die all over again and he wanted to prevent her having the same fate. The explosions of rifle fire meant that his warning went unheard.

The very minute Beth-Ann raised her head to move to the aid of her wounded husband, it was all but blown clean off her shoulders.

The children were crying openly now. Before, they'd whimpered, almost silently, but the sight of death and blood was more than they could comprehend. Joe hugged Eileen tightly, thinking it might be the last time he ever hugged a girl; it was certainly the first time. And even though the horror of their situation filled his head, he still felt stirrings he hadn't experienced before and felt ashamed of himself.

Ben, Bertram, Thadius and Patrick kept up a volley of shots, trying to keep their attackers pinned down as Joe, releasing Eileen and telling her to stay well down and behind him, began pulling Doug by his booted feet backwards and out of the line of fire.

The three attackers could sense the shots coming at them had reduced and one of them got a rush of blood to his head. Scrambling to his feet, he made a charge towards the wagons, firing his Winchester from the hip and yelling like a banshee.

The noise, the unexpected charge and the fusillade of shots coming from his rifle, momentarily stunned the four settlers and they watched, open mouthed, as the man came closer.

Ben Dowie was the first to regain his senses. Taking careful aim, sweat pouring down his face in a torrent, he squeezed the trigger of his brand new Winchester rifle.

It seemed to go deathly silent as the shell exploded and the bullet shot out of the long barrel. For a second, Ben was sure he could see the slug, flying through the air, dead in line with its target.

The charging man was oblivious to his fate; he was still yelling and shooting as the slug ripped into his chest, sending a spray of crimson into the air just as the man catapulted backwards.

The look of surprise was the one thing Ben would remember. It was as if the man had never even dreamed that these settlers could come anywhere near him.

His flight backwards went in slow motion. Both arms flew up, the rifle went off once before it sailed fifteen feet into the air, landing harmlessly in the dirt. Ben could see the man had left the ground, legs and arms loose, like the rag doll Eileen always used to carry around with her.

He landed in the dirt and a small cloud of dust rose, then settled slowly.

The shooting stopped.

With the exception of heavy breathing, and the sobs coming from the children, it was silent.

Bertram Dowie gave a whoop and slapped his son on the back, congratulating him on his shot. He forgot about the other two gunmen. He died with a smile on his face, soaking Ben with his blood.

Patrick and Thadius were shocked out of their joy and began to fire again.

Ben, his head resting on his dead father's shoulder, sobbed quietly, then he, too, picked up his rifle, gritted his teeth, and then emptied the chamber of his Winchester. The click, click of the hammer told him the gun was empty, but he kept pulling the trigger anyway.

It was Joe who handed him Doug's rifle; poking his father on the shoulder with the barrel, he reached forward and took the empty gun to reload it.

Ben turned to look at his fourteen-year-old son and realized, in that moment, that the boy was becoming a man. He smiled reassuringly at Joe who smiled back, then Ben commenced to shooting again with a greater sense of purpose – and aim.

The two remaining bandits were now having second thoughts about the wisdom of their attack.

Although they'd done this sort of thing many times in the past, it was the first time they'd ever suffered any casualties. Maybe they *thought* they were invincible, now they *knew* they weren't.

A withdrawal was required. Slowly, leaving their dead partner where he'd fallen, they began to edge away from the wagons and make their way back to the horses.

Ben, Patrick and Thadius saw them making their escape and inwardly breathed a sigh of relief. The fight was over, at least for the moment. The three discussed whether they should pursue their attackers or get the hell away.

It was Ben who made up their minds for them.

There wasn't any point in running away, he'd told them. With the wagons, they couldn't outrun them. They could pick them off any time they chose. They had to go after them. Finish this thing once and for all.

Reluctantly, the other two men agreed. Ben told them to keep shooting, try and make their getaway as difficult as they could while he unhitched the horses and saddled up.

Patrick and Thadius, with Joe reloading, began to fire at the retreating men. Pretty soon, it proved useless, as a small bluff covered their escape, presumably, they thought, where their wounded accomplice held the reins of their animals.

Ben worked as fast as he could, but, just as he was no marksman, he was no horseman, either. The animals were already spooked to high hell and back and it was only the rickety brakes on the wagons that was between them and galloping off at breakneck speed, leaving what remained of the three families high and dry.

Ben worked feverishly with the leathers, the animals rearing. Even though he spoke to them in soothing tones, it made no difference. If it was their co-operation he was after, they were in no mood to give it.

The two bandits made good their escape. Thadius and Patrick, now standing upright in front of the lead wagon, loosed off as many shots as they could manage. They didn't score another hit on the men though, but they did manage to bring down the empty horse of the dead man.

Neither Thadius nor Patrick was certain who'd hit what, but, as they watched, the animal regained its footing and, saddleless, stampeded after the other three.

Patrick ran forwards, firing from the hip ineffectively. The three riders disappeared in a cloud of dust. Reaching the bluff, Patrick saw the old leather saddle lying in the dirt and for the life of him, he felt he had to pick it up.

The strap securing the saddle to the horse was clean bust. It seemed a bullet had scored through it, maybe winging the horse at the same time.

Lugging it back, Patrick stopped at the body of the dead man. His face, mouth and eyes wide open, stared back sightlessly at him, the surprised look still there.

His chest was just red. Blood had soaked through and run down into the dirt and already, a swarm of flies, attracted by the fresh blood, began to settle on and around the corpse.

Patrick tasted bile as he looked down at the man, but he felt no sympathy. They'd killed too many of his own. On impulse, he kicked out at the dead man, sending a cloud of flies into the air, where they hovered just for a few seconds, before returning to their feast.

Ben gave up on the horses. It was too much for a man to do on his own. He hung his head and, as Martha went to his side, the grief and strain of the past few days were more than he could endure.

Unashamedly, tears rolled down his cheeks and sobs racked his body.

Joe ran to his father's side to join his mother, they were all that was left of their family.

The stunned silence of the three groups, each mourning the deaths of their own, was a sight Ben would never forget.

Pulling himself together, he told Martha to attend to Doug. Then he grabbed shovels and a pick-axe from the lead wagon and, without issuing an order to the other men, he began digging.

*   *   *

'Cows are ready, Mr Dowie,' Hank Jodes, foreman

of Broken Saddle, said to his boss.

'Men ready to roll?' Ben asked.

'Ready, willin' an' able,' Hank replied. 'Shouldn't take no more than two weeks to reach the stockade. Chow's stashed and Ole Maggot's chompin' at the bit to get off.'

'Let 'em roll,' Ben said. 'I'll see you in three weeks' time.'

'I'm gone,' Hank said, replaced his stetson and left the office.

Ben Dowie sat at his mahogany desk, a pen in his hand hovering over paperwork. Paperwork, he thought, bane of my life.

Martha entered the office carrying a tray with two mugs and a pot of fresh coffee.

'Thought you might need a break,' she said as she placed the tray on the desk.

Ben smiled. Even after thirty years of marriage, she still sent shivers down his spine when she smiled at him. Standing, he crossed to the front of his desk and hugged his wife.

'Coffee would be nice,' he said and released her.

Martha filled the two mugs and handed Ben one.

'The drive off?' she asked.

'Just. Hank's riding with 'em this time, I think he feels a bit stifled here at times.' Ben paused. 'Come to think of it, so do I. Seems this damn paperwork gets more an' more every day.'

'That's what makes the bank happy,' Martha said. 'Paperwork and plenty of it.'

Ben smiled. 'Where's Joe?'

'Well, I think he's gone along with Hank. You know those two are inseparable,' Martha said and waited for the fireworks.

'If I've told that boy once, I've told him a thousand times,' Ben began, but he didn't get any further.

'Ben, he is *not* a boy. He's twenty-three years-old, he's a man. You know how good he is with the cattle. He loves the thrill of the drive.' Martha watched her husband's face closely, to see if she was getting through.

'I know what he loves,' Ben said eventually. 'But if he ever harbours any hopes of taking over the Broken Saddle, he's got to know a helluva lot more than ramrodding steers!'

Martha stayed silent; not through fear, but she studied her husband of thirty years intently. A proud man, she'd only ever seen him cry twice; once when they'd finished burying their youngest son, Billy, all those years ago, and, on the same day after the gunfight.

His hair was still as black as the ace of spades and his penetrating brown eyes had lost none of their sparkle. There were a few more wrinkles, laughter lines, he called them, but that was all. His body was still lean and firm even though he was rapidly reaching fifty-five.

'He has plenty of time to learn,' Martha said. 'Plenty of time.'

*   *   *

Patrick Malloy had opted for sheep. His farmstead, Blarney Farm, a name he thought was funny, backed on to Ben's and although cowmen had traditionally treated sheep-herders, as they called them, along with a few choice other names that were less than complimentary, the two men were firm friends.

Martha and Siobhan, as well as Pat junior and Eileen, were bonded as one family. Both mothers hankered after Joe and Eileen getting wed. They'd been sweethearts ever since that day in the desert, but it never got any more serious than being the best of friends.

Patrick ran nearly three-thousand head of sheep, and although there was a fence between the two farms, the bane of cattlemen everywhere, there was no animosity. In fact, Ben and his family welcomed fresh lamb on their table as much as Patrick and his family enjoyed fresh beef.

Pat junior worked as hard, if not harder than his father. Planting seed, the corn had been his idea, and, using the seed-potatoes they'd brought over from Ireland, he'd managed several good crops of Irish potatoes.

Eileen, when she worked, helped Siobhan around their spacious ranch-house. They employed ten people, including the only real casualty of their trip out West, Doug Cartwright.

Doug had never got over losing his wife and, as soon as his wound had healed, had taken to the bottle.

For a year, the Malloys and the Dowies could

only stand by and watch helplessly as Doug seemed intent on drinking himself to death.

Then one day, he stopped. Just like that. No fanfare, no fuss. He'd not taken a drop of alcohol for four years and his youthful appearance was slowly but surely returning.

Doug divided his time between the two ranches. He became an expert horseman and liked nothing better than breaking in fresh broncos, always teaching them to roll over and play dead. Once he'd achieved that, the animal was as tame as a kitten.

The families had done well. The land they'd purchased from the Government had suited their purposes and, although they had decided to get on with their lives, the memory of the trip out West was constantly with them.

So when the three cowboys rode in to Blarney Farm looking for work, Patrick didn't hesitate to hire them on the spot and get them fence-posting before they had a chance to unroll their blankets.

It was a decision he would regret.

TWO

It took nearly an hour for the three men to dig the graves. The ground, sandy and rocky, did not aid their shovels and picks. Neither did their broken hearts.

In a neat row, beside the already buried Billy Dowie, stretched three more graves: Beth-Ann Cartwright, Bertram Dowie and Seamus and Margaret Malloy, buried as they had lived, together.

Gently, the bodies were lowered into their final resting places. Wrapped in tarpaulins from one of the wagons – Ben couldn't see the point now in taking all three wagons, they covered their remains with sand. Then Ben and Patrick piled rocks onto the sandy mounds in an effort to stop wolves or polecats from digging them up again.

High above, buzzards were riding the thermals, keeping their death-cold eyes on their movements. The smell of blood filled the air.

When they had finished, Ben said a few words from the Good Book, choking back tears as he read. Then each in turn gave a silent prayer and one after the other began to question the sense in carrying on.

As was usually the case, it was the women who had the strength of feeling to motivate their menfolk. Stressing the need to continue their journey, otherwise the killings would have been for nothing.

It took the men a while to come to their senses: each had lost a loved one and in reality their deaths were only just sinking in. The horror of the past couple of hours was now being relived mentally, second by second.

Martha finished dressing Doug's wound, but she could tell from his eyes that it wasn't the slug in his shoulder that was slowly killing him. He couldn't take his eyes off the makeshift cross that was all that remained of his young bride.

His mind, tormented beyond belief, went over and over again the plans they had made, the children they would have and the love they shared.

Now, it was all gone, and would *never* return. His heart beat like stone over the bottomless pit that was his stomach and, at that point, Doug Cartwright lost all hope.

Thadius Malloy was only slightly better off, at least he didn't have a slug to contend with. He'd buried his brother and sister-in-law, and now the only family he had left – outside of Ireland – was Patrick and his family.

Thadius sighed. It will take a while, he thought, to get over this sorry lot.

Ben decided to unload the Cartwright wagon and spread Doug's possessions between the other two, the horses he hitched up behind his own lead wagon.

Getting no response from Doug at all, he sorted out himself what should be taken and what he'd leave behind.

Thadius walked across to help and Patrick, who had been keeping guard while the graves were dug and the wagon unloaded, just in case the badmen decided to give it another go, joined them and within fifteen minutes, the job was done.

'There's nothing more we can do here,' Ben said solemnly.

'Except burn the wagon,' Patrick said. 'I'd hate to see those bastards get anything from what's left behind.'

Again, there was no response from Doug Cartwright, so Ben took it upon himself to fire the wagon.

With everyone now aboard the two wagons, Ben ignited the Cartwright wagon and stood back, making sure it caught, before climbing aboard his own.

Thick black smoke curled into the air as the wagon caught, and the sound of crackling wood and hisses broke the deathly silence.

Grabbing the reins of his team, Ben picked up the whip stashed on the running board and cracked it over his horses. The two-wagon train set off.

No one turned round.

The passage was slow, there seemed no need to hurry.

Martha tried desperately to keep spirits high, even though tears welled, uncried, in her eyes as she thought of her dead son.

The terrain began to change as they made their way West. They skirted the desert, leaving behind trees, grass and landmarks of any description.

Ben, full of confidence when he'd left Boston, now began to feel the power of the country. The only point of reference was the sun, which slowly began to sink in the western sky.

There had been wagon trains leaving Boston, almost weekly, but the three families couldn't afford the fees. Although, presumably safer than travelling alone, after they'd all stocked up, bought wagons, horses and the final instalment on the land purchased from the government, there was precious little left.

The jittery stomach Ben had felt, as self-appointed leader of the little group, when they were attacked, now returned as the enormity of their journey hit home.

It was the first time any of them had seen, let alone been in a desert, and Ben was determined to stay on the edge for as long as possible. He felt it was their last link with civilization.

The sand, rippled from the wind, seemed ever moving. Ben was concerned that if they set off into it, the wagons would get bogged down and they'd be stranded.

With a great feeling of unease, Ben gritted his

teeth. Everyone was looking to him to get them to their promised land.

* * *

Hank Jodes rode point on the herd as it pulled out of the north pasture of Broken Saddle. Beside him rode Joe Dowie, a grin on his face wider than the Colorado River.

Behind them, spread out over a half mile wide and two miles long, walked the steers they'd taken a year to raise, and were now headed to Flagstone and the biggest cattle market outside Los Angeles.

'Beautiful day, Hank,' Joe said.

'Sure is, Joe. One o' the best. If this weather keeps up, the trip'll pass in no time.'

'I don't *want* the trip to pass quick,' Joe said. 'Pa's intent on me takin' over the ranch, an' he thinks I should be stuck behind a desk, figurin' paperwork.'

'Your Pa's right, Joe. Ain't no future in ramrodding. Them there steam engines is getting closer an' closer an' purty soon, all we'll be a-doin' is shunting them cows up a ramp.'

'But there's still ropin' and brandin' and fencin',' Joe said.

'A man can get tired mighty easy doin' them sort o' jobs, Joe.'

'But it's outside. Out in the fresh air. I ain't gonna spend the rest o' my life stuck behind a desk. An' that's a fact.'

Both men were silent for a while. The beauty of the countryside was awe-inspiring. To the north, the Sierra Nevada mountains grew out of the desert floor, seeming to provide an impenetrable barrier. To the south and east, the desert stretched for as far as the eye could see.

The sky was a brilliant blue, with white, fluffy clouds that seemed to be sitting atop the mountains. The sun, bright yellow, so bright you couldn't look at it without slamming your eyes closed, burned down unmercifully, its reflected light and heat rising up from the sand.

The cattle, fed and watered that morning, were content; but Hank knew better than to rely on that being the case as the day progressed. He'd been on drives where guns had shot off accidentally, and the steers hadn't batted an eyelid.

On others, a sidewinder may have crossed the path of the lead steer and the whole herd had been panicked into a stampede that had taken hours to quieten down, and days to round up loose steers.

Trouble was, whenever you got a stampede, you got dead cattle: those that couldn't run as fast as the rest of the herd were trampled to death. Some just plain up and died in panic.

'What you thinkin' on, Hank?' Joe asked.

'Hell, I was jus' recalling some of the drives I've been on. That's all.'

'Tell me about 'em.'

'Hell, not much to tell. Hardship, mostly. Had a few laughs though. Pulls folks together. Adversity, they calls it.'

'But what about Indians, rustlers an' stuff like that?'

'We had a few. Used to leave a steer or two for the Injuns anyways. Most of 'em were starvin' to death. They didn't wanna kill anybody, jus' wanted to eat.

'Seems most o' the buffalo up north bin kilt off by trappers. Heard tales of miles of rottin' bodies, skinned and left for the buzzards. One thing 'bout them Injuns, they only kill what they need to eat.'

'You ever fight 'em?' Joe asked, a brightness shining in his eyes.

'Nope. Never have. Never want to, neither. Reckon we can live together, 'ventually.'

The two rode in silence fora while, Hank keeping his eyes peeled, checking the lead bull. The breeze was brushing into their faces and, although warm, it felt cooling in comparison to the unrelenting heat that barrelled down on them.

To the rear of the herd, it was another story. The gentle breeze was enough to raise a dust cloud from the thousands of hooves ahead. A great pall of yellow, cloying, choking dust hung in the air, reluctant to sink back down again.

Cowboys wore their bandannas tied tightly over nose and mouth in an attempt to stop the sand particles clogging up their throats. But no matter how tightly they tied them, the dust found a way through.

Visibility, too, was a problem. Sometimes you couldn't see your hand in front of your face.

'Reckon I'll check out the rear,' Hank said reluctantly.

'I'll go,' Joe said.

'You can come along if 'n you want. But it ain't no picnic back there.'

* * *

Patrick Malloy had watched as the great herd slowly made its way eastwards. The great pall of dust would soon be arriving at his front door, as it always did. He was grateful he only ever drove his sheep west, straight in to Los Angeles. The prairie was a damn sight easier to navigate than the desert.

Turning, he made his way back to the ranch-house. Time for breakfast.

Siobhan was busy over the range, the kitchen filled with the aroma of ham and fresh eggs, and there was bread rising in the oven. Already seated at the table were Pat junior and Eileen, looking as pretty as a picture.

'Good day to you all,' Patrick said as he entered. He walked straight to the washbasin, splashed water on his ruddy face, dried it and sat, as was his custom, at the head of the large family table that was set slap-bang in the centre of the giant kitchen Siobhan had demanded was necessary.

'Good morning, father,' Eileen said and leant across the corner of the table, planting a kiss on his cheek.

'And how are you, young Pat?' Patrick asked his son.

'Hungry,' came the almost sullen answer of a

typical nineteen-year-old.

Patrick ignored the reply. For him, breakfast, surrounded by his family, was the best time of any day.

Looking through the window, he saw his hands making their way to the bunkhouse after the early morning chores.

His flocks were grazing peaceably enough, it took a lot to rile them – unlike cattle – and as long as they had grass to chew on they were content.

'I'm going out riding after breakfast,' Eileen said, 'if that's all right?'

'Just as long as you don't go too far,' her mother replied. Siobhan Malloy was standing by the hot plates, beside her a large pile of cooked ham, crisp and golden. She was just finishing off the eggs and at the same time checking on the day's bread and the biscuits for breakfast.

'Anything I can do?' Eileen asked.

'Sure, you can eat it when it's in front of you,' her mother said.

When Siobhan was cooking, all the conversation was directed at her back, hers to the range.

She brought the plates of ham and eggs over to the table and set them in the middle, then took out a loaf and a tin pan full of biscuits and placed them next the other food. Before sitting at the table, she placed all the cutlery and dishes she'd been using in the kitchen sink; a large, rectangular iron sink she'd insisted on bringing out from Boston, despite its weight and size.

Then, satisfied that everything was as it should

be, she sat at the opposite end of the table, facing her husband.

'We thank thee, Lord, for the good food placed in front of us, amen,' Patrick intoned.

A chorus of amens followed and the eating began.

*   *   *

There were no prayers of thanks out in the bunkhouse. The men moved single-file past the long table, helping themselves to breakfast. The three newcomers were last in line and, when they'd filled their plates and helped themselves to coffee, they kept very much to themselves.

Martin O'Flynn, foreman of the Blarney, as the ranch/farm was known to all and sundry, eyed the three men with a certain amount of suspicion, but then, he eyed nearly everyone who wasn't of Irish descent that way.

He reasoned that if Mr Malloy had hired them, they must be all right, but he had a nagging doubt in the back of his ginger-haired head that wouldn't leave him alone.

Sure, he thought, they'd worked well that morning; no complaints on that score, to be sure.

But. Martin O'Flynn was full of buts, and until he could shed them, he didn't trust a soul.

He sat alone eating his food, but his eyes rarely left the three men. They all looked like any other cowboy: unshaven, dust-covered clothes of indeterminate age and colour. Their gunbelts were a mite lower slung than most, but there was nothing unusual about that. Many men wore their sideirons low down, it didn't mean they were shootists, but it didn't mean they weren't, either.

As he stared, one of the men caught his eye. O'Flynn felt a slight shiver run down his back as he stared into the almost black eyes that showed no sign of an expression at all. They were dead eyes that stared back/him, dead eyes in an expressionless face.

The 'but' word came back into O'Flynn's mind, and this time, it wouldn't go away.

THREE

The sun finally fell away behind the distant horizon and Ben Dowie knew they'd better camp up for the night.

As the sun dipped, so a chill began to fill the air. The heat coming up from the sun and the cold air above made crazy lines in the sky, sometimes only ten feet off the ground and Ben's eyes did a war-dance as his peripheral vision caught sight of something that, when he turned to look at it, vanished.

He realized he was spooking himself and reined in.

The two wagons were parked side-by-side and, using wood they'd brought with them or found out on the trail, Patrick set young Pat the task of building a fire.

'You think that wise?' Ben asked.

'Hell, if we don't have no fire, we'll freeze,' Patrick said.

'If we *do* have a fire, those bandits might come back,' Ben said uneasily.

'Ben,' Patrick started, 'if those bandits decide to

come back they got tracks a mile wide to follow. They won't need the light of a fire to find us.'

Ben thought about that. Patrick was right. If they wanted to find them he guessed it would be easy enough.

'I'll stand watch,' Ben said. 'How about we take it three hours at a time throughout the night?'

'Suits me, Ben. As long as we get to eat first,' Patrick smiled.

'Always thinking of your stomach,' Siobhan said as she pulled out boxes and sacks from the back of the wagon.

'Man cannot live on love alone,' Patrick said to his wife and grabbed her round the waist, hugging her tightly as if realizing how lucky they were to be still alive.

Young Pat piled the wood and got the matches from the wagon and, as the dry timber crackled, it seemed to bring a certain normality back into their lives.

Martha and Siobhan busied themselves with preparing supper, while the men kept a watchful eye out before they ate, then they'd take turns in standing guard.

Ben went to his wagon, retrieved his tobacco and lit up his pipe. Martha hated that pipe more than anything else in the world, but he loved it.

As he puffed clouds of blue smoke into the air, he saw the broken saddle resting on the boards of Patrick's wagon.

'What the hell you fetch this thing for?' Ben asked.

'To be sure, I don't know,' Patrick said. 'It just seemed like I had to pick it up.'

Ben studied the saddle then ran his fingers across the hard, worn leather. He wondered if the man who'd ridden this saddle was the same man who'd killed his father?

'Would you mind if I had this?' he asked Patrick.

'Sure, an' why would I mind? If you want it, have it with me compliments.'

'Thanks.'

There was nothing special or valuable about the saddle, it was an ordinary cowboy saddle, weather- and sweat-stained, dark brown leather.

But there was something to the feel of the leather, the studding, the broken belly-strap, that made Ben think of it as a symbol. Of what, he didn't know, but he had to have it.

They ate supper, grouped round the campfire. The men ate hurriedly and silently, eyes switching this way and that, ears pricked for the slightest sound and, surprisingly, the desert at night was full of noises: scamperings, swishes, the howl of wolf or coyote.

When the meal was finished and the women and children automatically began to clear the dishes away, cleaning off the tin plates and the stewpot with sand, Ben filled the coffeepot, bade his children good night, and settled down again by the fire for a smoke and a coffee.

Martha and Siobhan soon retired, their day having already been longer with three lots of cooking and cleaning.

Patrick sat opposite Ben with Thadius seating himself in the middle. The men didn't talk, they sipped coffee and almost subconsciously, looked over each others' shoulders, peering into the blackness of the desert night.

The moon, shielded by high-flying cloud, shed little light. What light there was was silvery-blue and cold, as was the air. When the men breathed out, a fine cloud of vapour was visible, even close by the fire.

Ben finished his pipe, drained the last dregs of his coffee and stood. He was on first watch. So he bade Patrick and Thadius goodnight, telling Patrick he'd wake him in three hours – all being equal.

Both men unrolled their beds and settled in beneath the wagons. Ben stoked up the campfire, picked up his Winchester and, rather than stay seated, began to pace around the wagons.

Then he stopped walking: it suddenly struck him that he'd be better out of the campsite, the brightness of the fire was affecting his night vision and, besides, there was no way he could have an unrestricted three-hundred and sixty-degree view of the suroundings. The two wagons blocked his view north and the campfire the south.

Telling Patrick what he was going to do and where he'd be, Ben set off to look for a good spot.

It didn't take long. A slight rise in the desert floor, atop a small dune, was ideal. He sat down, scanning the area 'til his eyes began to water. He knew he'd have to do something or he'd fall asleep.

Away from the fire, it was both cold and dark, but his night vision was getting better by the minute. The night sky to the west was much brighter than he'd imagined it would be and Ben knew he could use that as a sight line. Anyone approaching from the west, either afoot or on horse, would be silhouetted. If they approached from the east, they'd have to cross the campfire glare.

He decided to study his new rifle. Martha had been against him buying it. She couldn't see the need for it, but Ben had insisted. He'd bought a Winchester lever-action .45–75. The salesman had particularly recommended the weapon as the same size slugs would also fit his Colt Peacemaker.

The salesman had been good. He'd pointed out to Martha that a weapon *was* a necessity, against both man and animal, but particularly animal. He'd laboured that point to Ben's wife almost giving her the impression that a grizzly lived behind every rock *and* a rattlesnake underneath. In the end, Martha had to agree. A gun maybe was necessary. But she couldn't see the sense in buying a rifle, which in itself, at twenty-seven dollars, was a major investment on their meagre budget, *and* a handgun that cost almost as much.

Again, the salesman patiently explained that you could draw and shoot an object at close range far quicker with a handgun. On the other hand, an object in the distance could be hit more accurately by the rifle.

Martha was about to question the need to shoot *anything* that distant but, much as it went against the grain, she reluctantly agreed and Ben Dowie had his first two guns. He purchased bullets and a cleaning kit, as well. The salesman had stressed the importance of keeping both weapons clean. Further stating it was preferable to clean them every time after use, as the black powder used in the shells soon built up. And, although neither the Colt nor the Winchester were anywhere near as dangerous as some of the suicide specials that one or two of the more disreputable gun shops tried to foist off on unsuspecting travellers, there was still an element of danger in *any* weapon that wasn't looked after.

Ben smiled to himself, that salesman *had* been good. He'd have to be to convince Martha to part with just over fifty-eight dollars and change. Using the cleaning kit, Ben began to clean the rifle. The salesman had shown him how to dismantle it, but that had been nearly three weeks ago, and Ben hadn't tried to do it yet and, as it was dark, he wasn't about to try now.

The oil-soaked cleaning-cloth left a fine coating over the barrel and lever-action and Ben was careful not to let it get covered in sand.

Every few seconds, he raised his head to peer into the desert, his ears alert to any sound.

When the scream erupted, it almost made Ben jump out of his skin.

*   *   *

Gradually, the farmhands began to filter out of the bunkhouse: some to tend the fields as the corn was near its second harvest, the rest to fix fences, break or exercise the horses or move the sheep to pastures new.

The three newcomers were detailed to ride the fence, their task to find and repair any damage.

This suited the three down to the ground for their purposes. Out on their own, unsupervised, and left to their own devices.

They saddled up after receiving their orders from O'Flynn and set off in a northerly direction. When they were out of sight of the farmhouse, they altered course, heading south-east with their eyes fixed firmly on the distant dust-cloud.

*   *   *

Eileen Malloy helped her mother clean away the breakfast dishes, fed the chickens and picked up the two or three eggs that had been laid since her mother had been to collect breakfast eggs at dawn. All this to ease her conscience as she intended to be out for the rest of the day at least.

Joe Dowie had told her he was riding with the drive and Eileen planned to surprise him.

Although she hadn't told her parents, she did, unfortunately, tell the stable lad the day before of her intentions, so that he could get her horse ready.

The lad had been sworn to secrecy. She told him not to tell her mother or father – especially her father, as he would keep her in the house as sure as eggs were eggs. But young Jody, the stablehand, hadn't been told not to tell anyone else, and he was overheard at supper on the previous night and a plan had been hatched.

Saying goodbye as she left the house, Eileen heard the call of her mother telling her not to ride out too far and be back by mid-afternoon at the *latest* or else there'd be hell to pay.

Eileen smiled. The only thing she was thinking of was the look on Joe's face when she turned up!

Her horse was ready when she entered the stable. The side-saddle her father had given her for her birthday just two weeks ago, still needed breaking in but the jet black leather with silver studs looked magnificent against the gentle gold of her palomino. Her father had insisted that genteel ladies *always* rode side-saddle.

Thanking Jody for getting the horse ready and in such beautiful condition, she stroked her horse's coat and the animal nuzzled her face in pleasure. Jody locked his fingers together and boosted Eileen into the saddle.

The boy stood back – boy, but seventeen and tall for his age, he had ideas on Eileen and, as she sat atop her horse, her long maroon riding skirt spread behind her, her black jacket and waistcoat topped off with a black ladies' stetson, his heart almost missed *two* beats.

Smiling as only a woman in love can, Eileen

gently tapped the mare's neck and at a walk, she set off the find Joe, her childhood, and still, sweetheart.

Little did Jody know that he'd never see her again.

FOUR

By the time Ben Dowie reached the campsite, everyone was awake and standing round Thadius Malloy.

The old man was lying prone on the ground where he'd fallen and Patrick was just turning him over.

'What the hell happened?' Ben asked, his face filled with concern.

'By all the saints, I don't know,' Patrick replied without looking up.

The old man was almost delirious, muttering incoherently as Patrick rolled him over onto his back. Thadius' face was ashen, even in the dim light of the campfire and Patrick saw that all he could see were the whites of his eyes, the pupils either staring downwards or straight up.

'Thad? Thad, can you hear me?' Patrick asked.

Thadius made no reply or response except that his eyes closed.

Patrick looked at every inch of exposed skin on Thadius, face, neck, hands even rolling Thadius's trousers up to check if anything had bitten him.

He found nothing.

Patrick leaned right over Thadius's face, trying to feel breath.

'I can't feel his breath,' he said.

Ben knelt down and placed two fingers on Thadius's neck. There was no pulse.

'Patrick, he's dead!' Ben said somberly.

Patrick stared at his uncle. 'I don't believe it,' he said slowly and lowered his head. 'The sea journey, the bother we had getting from that New York place to Boston, those bandits, he survived the lot. Now, he just dies.'

'Siobhan, I think you better get the children back to bed, there's no need for them to go through any more'n they have to.' Ben placed a hand on Patrick's shoulder, there was no need for words.

'Guess he just had a heart attack,' Ben said consolingly.

Both men stood and walked to the wagon. They hadn't expected to be digging yet another grave.

Wrapping Thadius up in cloth, they lifted him and carried the body to the shallow grave. The sand was too fine for any depth. Every time they dug their shovels into the grave, the sand ran freely back again.

With Patrick and Siobhan, Ben and Martha in attendance, they paid their last respects.

After taking his wife back to their wagon, checking on Joe, Ben resumed his guard duty. It would be a lot longer than the agreed three hours, but, if necessary, Ben was prepared to stand guard all night.

It was two hours later when Patrick joined him.

'Can't sleep none,' Patrick had said. 'Thought I'd come an' relieve you.'

'How's Siobhan?' Ben asked.

'Okay, I guess. It kinda numbs you after a while. All this killin' an' death. I haven't taken none of it in yet, to be sure,' Patrick replied.

'We still got a ways to go, yet,' Ben said dourly.

'I know, and that worries the hell out of me, I can tell you. Any more days like this and there won't be none of us left by the time we get there,' Patrick said.

The two men fell silent, both lost in thought. Around them the night-time desert breathed. The breeze, cold on their hands and faces, whispered across the sand making subtle alterations to the ripples. The night sky, black and forbidding was punctuated by a myriad of twinkling stars that disappeared, only to reappear as some distant, high up and unseen cloud passed in front of them. The moon, in its first quarter, shone down with a watery light that flickered, giving the living sand a ghost-like quality.

The mirages of the day were replaced by the ghosts of night. Dark shadows, blacker than the prevailing blackness, swept across the desert floor like approaching death.

* * *

The bleeding had stopped by the time the three badmen had reached a small waystation.

The slug had ripped into the shoulder and gone straight through, leaving a hole as it scraped off the shoulder blade and exited. No major blood vessels had been hit, otherwise the man would be dead by now.

The aching had given way to a dull throb that was intensified each time his mount hit the ground.

Now, sliding out of the saddle, the pain eased up some.

The three, Dan Stacey, Luke Palmer and Harley Young, were as mad as hell. Harley in particular. It was his older brother, Slim, they'd left out there in the desert.

Harley was all for setting off and finishing the job, but it was the cool head of Luke that had prevented the younger man from joining his brother.

The waystation was manned by husband and wife, Harold and Aggie Carter, employees of the stage company that served the outlying districts of Boston supplying everything from mail to food, grain to fancy goods.

Aggie dressed the wound in Dan's shoulder, telling him how lucky he'd been that the robbers, who'd attacked the three, hadn't been better shots else he'd be a dead 'un.

It was Luke who'd thought up the story. You couldn't stop folk being inquisitive, and Luke's brain was quicker that most.

Bandaged, fed and watered, the three men rested in the parlour, while Harold volunteered to feed and water their horses.

Aggie came in and offered more coffee, which the three gratefully accepted. Aggie left them saying she had to get food ready as the stage was due in in an hour.

Luke grinned from ear to ear, showing blackened stumps of teeth.

'What the hell you a-grinnin' fer?' Harley asked.

'You heard what the lady said?' he replied.

'Yeah, she's gonna do some cookin',' Harley muttered.

' 'Cause the stage is a-comin'.' Luke waited for the dime to drop. It didn't.

'Sometimes I wonder what in blazes goes on in between your ears,' Luke said.

'I ain't a-thinkin' none too straight,' Harley said. 'We jus' left Slim out there.'

'Ain't nothin' we could do fer him. Damn fool, chargin' in the way he did.'

Harley stood his handgun seemed to jump from his holster in a smooth, silky action.

'You callin' Slim a fool?' Harley said menacingly. 'You take that back.'

Luke sat where he was, a look of disdain on his face.

'I'm a-talkin' to you, Luke.'

'I know it. An' I don't take nothin' back. If 'n Slim had stayed where he was, we'd be headed back to Boston with three wagons by now, 'stead o' sittin' here twiddling our fingers.'

'Slim weren't no fool.'

'He's dead, ain't he?' Luke said.

There was no reply from Harley. A look of sadness flitted across his face for a second before his brows knitted together in puzzlement. 'What you sayin' 'bout the stage?'

Luke looked skywards and breathed out deeply. 'We wasted our time out there,' he began, keeping it simple for Harley to follow. 'We ain't got diddly-squat for nearly two weeks work. The stage is a-comin' in. Now, what you suppose they got on that stage?'

'How the hell do I know?' Harley said.

'Well it ain't *too* difficult to work out none, now is it? You know as well as I do them stages take out the mail an' all sorts o' stuff. Well, I reckon we jus' help ourselves.'

'You mean rob the stage?' Harley asked.

'There, you see? I know'd you'd get there, 'ventually.'

Harley made for the door.

'Where the hell you goin'?' Luke asked.

'Gettin' ready,' Harley said.

'We got an hour, yet. Sit an' drink your coffee. No sense in runnin' off half-cocked. We got plenty o' time.' Luke picked up one of the tin mugs and damn near burned his lips off, the coffee was so hot. He didn't move a muscle though, that would have meant losing face.

Harley did as he was told. Sitting on the over-stuffed armchair, he sat right on the edge and his left leg was jumpin up and down like a drum roll at one of those fancy theatres Luke went to one time.

'Quit shakin' you damn leg up an' down,' Luke said. 'Fair drives me mad.'

'I ain't,' Harley said, and even as he said it, he looked down at his left leg as it thumped up and down. He stopped it.

'See, I ain't,' he repeated.

Luke just blew into his coffee to cool it down.

'Horses are fed an' watered,' Harold said, poking his head through the door but not coming into the parlour.

'Thanks, mister,' Luke said. 'How much we owe?'

'Hell, dollar a piece, I reckon,' Harold said. 'That includes the food.'

'Mighty good of you,' Luke said and handed over three dollar bills. Then he plucked another off the thin roll and gave Harold that, as well.

'Hey, thanks, mister,' a delighted Harold said. ' 'preciate that.'

'You're welcome,' Luke replied and the two shook hands.

'Well, be seein' you,' Harold said. 'Gotta get fresh horses ready. Stage's comin' in.' With that, he left.

'You givin' money away, now?' Harley said.

'I'll get it back later,' Luke said.

Dan Stacey started snoring – loudly.

'Fer God's sakes,' Luke said, and kicked Stacey's feet to wake him up or shut him up, whichever came first.

Stacey jumped, his eyes snapped open and a jolt of pain shot through his shoulder.

'What the hell you kickin' me fer?' he yelled.

'You're makin' too much noise, man can't think,' Luke said, not looking at Stacey.

'Check your weapons,' he went on. 'Make sure you got all six chambers loaded. I don't want no screw up this time.'

'What fer?' Stacey said.

'We's holdin' up the stage!' Harley grinned.

'Oh, shit!' Stacey said and proceeded to fall back to sleep.

Luke let him sleep. There was plenty of time. He lit a cigarette and drank his coffee as cool as you like.

From the kitchen came the sounds of plates being readied, pots and pans clanking together. From outside, the sound of horses, as Harold got a four-team ready to change over.

It was fifty-minutes' later when the stagecoach rolled to a halt.

Luke was already round the back of the waystation, on the pretext of using the toilet. Harley sat on the porch, a newspaper on his lap handgun ready. Stacey was in the window of the parlour, his handgun, drawn, hidden from the outside.

The dust settled and the driver and shotgun jumped to the ground. Atop the stage were bags and boxes all tied down under a rope net. There were more boxes and two crates strung to the rear.

Harold greeted the two men and pointed to the waystation where food and drink was ready for them, and then he began to unhitch the horses.

Luke appeared from the side of the waystation

and, holding his rifle at hip level, ordered the three men to halt and put their hands high.

They complied and Harley, throwing the newspaper to the ground, brought his handgun to bear.

'Now, throw your weapons down, real easy,' Luke said.

Harold was unarmed, the shotgun and driver drew their weapons and dropped them in the dirt.

The two men inside the stage drew their guns and waited for an opportunity.

'Where you want 'em, Luke?' Harley asked his partner.

'You damn fool. I should blow your head off now!' Luke growled.

'What I say?'

'You used my name, shit-head!'

The argument was just what the two men in the stagecoach needed. Unseen, they exited on the blind side, keeping low. One went to the rear, the other to the front.

The man with the tin star nodded and simultaneously, they both stood, Colts drawn and cocked.

'Drop it!' the man wearing the star ordered.

Luke was so mad at Harley that he'd allowed his concentration and guard to drop. He should have checked the stage.

'I said, drop your weapons!' the man ordered again.

From inside the waystation, Stacey blasted a hole through the window. The slug buried itself in the side of the stage.

At the same time, Luke and Harley hit the dirt, shooting as they went down.

The man wearing the star fired blindly through the shattered window and a cry rent through the air as the slug caught Stacey in the same shoulder he'd already been hit in. He collapsed to the floor, his cries continuing until he blacked out.

Harley and Luke began firing, but the shotgun and driver had regained their weapons and it didn't take them long to realize that if they didn't give up, they'd be dead men.

'Okay, okay,' Luke said. 'I'm droppin' my gun.'

Harley was silent.

'You too, mister!' tin star said.

'You want I should, Luke?' Harley said.

'Only if you wanna keep your head on yer shoulders,' Luke replied, already standing with his hands held high above his head.

Reluctantly, Harley released the hammer of his Colt and left it on the ground as he, too, stood up.

Both men from behind the stage emerged. The man wearing the star came forward, the other, dressed like a dandy, stayed where he was.

'Driver,' the tin star began, 'get me some rope.'

'You ain't a-fixin' no hangin' are you, mister?' the driver asked.

The man opened his jacket slightly to reveal to all the star he wore on his vest. 'Name's Garrett, Sheriff Pat F. Garrett, and you three men are under arrest,' was all he said.

Luke stood stunned. He'd heard that name

before. Now where the hell had he heard that name?

Then he remembered.

'Oh, shit!' Luke said.

'What? What's up Luke?' Harley asked.

The driver and shotgun as well as Harold began to laugh.

'You boys sure picked the wrong day an' the wrong stagecoach to rob,' the driver said, still laughing.

'What're they laughin' at?' Harley asked, a look of puzzlement on his face.

'Harley, you dumb sonuvabitch! This here's Sheriff Pat Garrett, don't that mean nothin'?' Luke said.

'Nope.'

'He's the man who killed Billy the Kid!'

FIVE

Eileen Malloy had always been a headstrong girl, maybe her experiences on the journey out West all those years ago had sculptured her personality, iron will and sense of purpose. Whatever it was, Eileen knew what she wanted and went after it like a bear to honey.

She was fed up with pussyfooting around with Joe Dowie and aimed to do something about it. Eileen had been in love with Joe since he'd first put his arm around her shoulders underneath the wagon all those years ago.

She felt that Joe loved her, too, but his love of the land and open air, and his fear of being tied down and stuck behind a desk had made her task less than easy.

With her long auburn hair flowing out behind her, Eileen cantered out of Broken Saddle, through the wooden archway that marked the entrance to the ranch and, as was the custom, she tapped the broken saddle that was fixed atop the wooden poles for luck.

Her father had told her the story of the saddle

many times, it being the one Patrick had given him all those years ago after ... well, she didn't like thinking about those days so she dismissed them from her thoughts.

The sun was shining, the sky was a clear blue and Eileen had never felt happier in her life. Today was the day that she and Joe would finally sort the rest of their lives out.

*   *   *

The small hut was located to the north of Broken Saddle and north-east of Blarney. Set in a small, dark canyon surrounded by rock, the hut was an ideal hideaway.

The three newcomers to the Malloy spread had holed out there for nearly two weeks before making their first move.

They'd found the hut by chance. Merely seeking high ground to camp out, they'd ridden into the blind canyon and couldn't believe their luck.

The roof needed fixing, but they set about that with an enthusiasm that was totally out of character. The cellar-door was all but rotted through, and they fashioned a new one. Supplies were brought in and stashed in a tarpaulin to the rear of the hut in a small cave, hardly big enough for a man to crawl inside, but big enough for the food. The last thing the three men wanted was to give the impression that the hut was occupied.

The three men were waiting on their visitor, and they knew he wouldn't let them down.

Jody, the young stable lad, had been promised a reward for his information. They'd conned him into giving them the information they wanted after overhearing his remarks about Eileen, and had arranged to meet him at noon.

Jody, young and gullible, had believed every word they'd told him. A surprise for Miss Malloy, they'd said; to help her with Joe, they'd said.

He entered the small canyon and reined in. The darkness and the change in temperature hit him full in the face and, for the first time, Jody had a sense of foreboding.

He stared at the hut through the gloom: there was no sign of movement, apart from the three horses tethered up outside. He couldn't see the pair of eyes that was watching him from the only window in the hut. A window that was dirt-smeared and cracked and almost impossible to see into.

Jody called out: 'Anyone there?'

Silence answered his call, that echoed off the canyon walls.

Telling himself off for getting so spooked, Jody dug his heels into his pony and walked on. The chill was getting through to him and he shivered as if someone had just walked over his grave.

He cast his eyes skywards. The clear, blue sky was refreshing to look at and reassuring. Reaching the tethering post, he dismounted and tied his pony to the pole.

There was no sound coming from inside the hut, not a light showing. Jody stepped onto the thin board that stuck out from the side of the hut and knocked, tentatively, on the badly-fitting door.

'Come in, kid,' a voice answered.

Jody pushed the door inwards. Inside, the darkness was complete, he couldn't see a thing.

'Hullo,' he said.

'Come on in,' the voice said again.

Jody took a step inside. He didn't see the log that smashed into his face, breaking practically every bone.

The force of the blow sent him flying through the air and he landed back outside, face up in the dirt.

'He dead?' another voice asked.

A man appeared through the doorway, the three-foot log still gripped in his grime-encrusted hands. He stood over the body of Jody, whose sightless eyes stared back through blood that was pooling in his sockets. Already, the dirt was stained red.

The man brought the log down once more full on what was left of Jody's face. There was a sickening crunch as his skull caved in and an even more sickening squelch as the log went through the bone and hit grey-matter.

'He is now,' the man replied and chuckled.

Two men emerged from the hut and stared down at the lifeless body.

'Git rid,' one of the men said.

The other two grunted their displeasure at having to move the bloody mess, but didn't voice anything.

Grabbing Jody by his legs, they dragged the body to the rear of the hut to a shallow grave that they'd already prepared. Unceremoniously, they dumped the body in.

One of the men went through the boy's pockets.

'Shit, he ain't even got a dime on him,' the man said disgustedly.

Then they began shovelling dirt into the hole. The surplus, they spread around so that there was not even a mound, then they trampled the dirt, compacting it so that within ten minutes it would be hard to tell anything untoward was there.

The bloodstained ground to the front of the hut had been cleaned up and anyone turning up in their absence would notice nothing.

Satisfied that all was secure, they even left the door to the hut open, then the three men mounted up and set off to put their plan in operation.

* * *

The drive had been going well. With the weather on their side, no chance of thunderheads, a drover's nightmare was thunder and lightning that could spook the steers and make a stampede unavoidable.

Joe was in his element: fresh air, at least riding point, good company, all the space in the world to ride in.

Hank Jodes was an old hand; nothing surprised him and he was ready for anything. Yet even he felt strangely relaxed. Whether it was because his boss's son was with him, he wasn't sure. One thing was sure, Hank was the trailboss, *not* Joe.

Fast approaching one in the afternoon, the first shift for grub were making their way forwards and towards Ole Maggot's chow wagon.

Ole Maggot – no one was really sure what his real name was – had been on more drives than most people had hot dinners. Maggot got his name from one particular drive along the Chisholm Trail, when the meat was so bad, dead maggots were found floating in the stew. He'd been the only person to eat it, saying it added flavour.

The wagon had gone on ahead some two hours previous and had set up a campsite to the side of the trail and upwind. Last thing Ole Maggot wanted was a dust cloud enveloping his wagon *and* his stew.

Thing is, you had to eat when you could, even when you weren't hungry; normally, back at the ranch, they wouldn't touch the stew with a branding iron, let alone a fork.

Reaching the wagon, the men settled in ones and twos and ate the food; they had no idea when they might get to eat again, so they crammed in as much as they could when they could.

It took only an hour for the start of the herd to pass by the campsite, by which time, the first shift had finished and Ole Maggot was ready for the rest of the boys.

So far, in the space of seven hours, sixteen cows had dropped a calf, three died but the rest were healthy enough. Two drovers took care of this

small group and travelled way back from the main
herd, while the calves got their footing, then every
time they got within striking distance of the herd,
another cow would give birth.

It was a chance most ranchers took: keeping the
pregnant cows back at the ranch, thereby losing
out on headage but gaining a calf, or taking the
risk that both cow and calf would survive the
journey and thereby increase the value of the
herd.

The small group kept the dust cloud in view as
they followed up. The choking dust continually
falling back to earth meant that both the men
guiding this small herd looked like bandits with
their bandannas tied tightly round their faces.

Eileen saw the small group ahead and decided
to bypass them. She didn't want the whole world
to know she was out there.

Cutting north, Eileen pushed her horse across
the path the herd had trampled out and was
certain that neither man had seen her passage.

She felt a thrill of excitement surge through her
body. She felt she was doing something illicit and
daring and that made her feel even better.

Along the north edge of the trail was a slight
rise, beyond that the land was flat and even. She
could travel ahead of the herd and, unless some of
the steers deviated, she could get past unseen.
She knew where Joe liked to ride; right up front.
She would park in the middle of the trail and
watch him approach.

*   *   *

The three riders also followed the trail left by the herd. They, too, cantered. Unhurried, but keeping up a steady pace, the three rode with purpose. They knew exactly what the Malloy girl was up to. They knew she planned to get to the front of herd unseen and their recce of the area over the previous two weeks, also told them to ride north of the trail. The south was open and flat and would mean too much of a detour.

The blue sky ahead was a dun colour as the dust rose from the drive. They knew they were less than thirty-minutes behind now. The girl, they reckoned, would be behind the rise, oblivious to the danger that stalked her.

The leader of the riders had a fixed grin on his face. Having spent ten years in a state penitentiary mainly breaking big rocks up into smaller ones on the chain gang, he could see the end in sight.

Ten years of hell, sweat and anger was about to be avenged. A red mist formed in front of the man's eyes as the anger returned and he had to fight hard to force it back inside.

Cutting across the trail, at more or less the same point as Eileen had, they crested the small rise and rode down the other side.

The front man reined in and peered into the distance. The sunlight, reflecting off the sand, made visibility difficult to say the least. The shimmering heat waves meant that anything in the distance was completely distorted.

Although not sure, the man felt he could see a lone rider. 'Come on,' he said. 'We're almost there.'

SIX

At the same time that Stacey, Palmer and Young were accompanying the legendary Pat Garrett back to Boston, the two wagons were well underway.

Dan's confidence was growing daily in his ability to both lead and see the journey through. But progress was slow.

In a way they were fortunate; having four spare horses, they could rotate the animals every two or three hours, but the penalty was that more horses meant more feed and water. With practice, the men had got the change-over down to ten minutes; two horses for the lead wagon and two for the other, but the days seemed to drag on interminably.

They reached the foot of the mountains just before dusk and Ben decided it would be foolish to continue in the dark, so they set up a base camp.

Patrick stood guard, they still feared the badmen would return, and the women prepared the food.

As night fell, they sat round a roaring campfire.

Wood was aplenty now, so they didn't have to stint on lumber.

Ben checked out their supplies: they had enough coffee to last them another month, dried goods in abundance now that their numbers had been forcibly reduced, but the thing they missed more than anything was fresh meat.

'I wonder what the wildlife is like in these parts?' Ben queried.

'Beats me,' Patrick replied, 'it's my first time, too.' He laughed at his own little joke.

'What say we go a-huntin'?' Ben suggested.

'Ah, well, now, that would be a good idea, but I'd probably shoot meself, or you in the process,' Patrick said. 'I'm not exactly Annie Oakley with the rifle.'

Ben laughed. Then, 'Joe? You'll come with me, will you?'

Joe's face lit up like a beacon. There was no way he'd refuse an offer like that.

Martha grunted and coughed, a preliminary to an objection.

'Now Martha,' Ben said. 'I know what you're going to say, but Joe's not a child any more, he's proved that on this journey. The west is wild, we all know that and the sooner he earns his first kill the better.'

'Besides,' Patrick chipped in, 'someone's got to stay here and guard the campsite. We don't want no marauders sneaking up on us.'

Whatever Martha was going to say, remained locked in her mouth. What the men had said was true. Joe had to learn to fend for himself.

'Very well,' she said. 'But you take good care of Joe. You're no Annie Oakley, either!'

Ben threw the dregs of his coffee to the ground and stood. Joe had already leapt to his feet in anticipation.

'Here, Joe,' Ben said to his son. 'Take this rifle. I'll run through how it works as we walk. Who knows, we could be eating rabbit for breakfast.'

Martha pulled a face. 'I don't think I *want* to be eating rabbit for breakfast.'

Martha, Siobhan and Eileen began to clear away the dishes. There was plenty of stew left which they would serve up for tomorrow's supper – unless, of course, they had something better.

Doug Cartwright remained as he had for the last two months: silent.

His wounds were healing nicely. There was no sign of infection, the thing that had worried Martha more than anything else. But there was no sign of him snapping out of his depression.

They had all tried to get him animated, but to little effect. He took no part in any discussion, offered no advice or help. He just sat where he was told to sit and held a now dog-eared photograph of his beloved Beth-Ann and stared at it for hours on end.

Martha and Siobhan were undecided as to what to do. They were tempted to steal the photograph while Doug slept. Maybe, they thought, if he didn't have her face to gaze at all the time, he'd snap out of it. But they couldn't bring themselves to be that heartless. They just waited for Doug to come through his grief the way they had.

Loaded with weapons and ammunition, Ben and Joe set off.

'If you hear two shots in rapid succession,' Ben said to Patrick, 'then we've got problems. Otherwise, if you hear gunfire, we'll be bringing home tomorrow's supper.'

'I'll keep watch,' Patrick said. 'I'll keep the campfire blazing, as well. Doesn't look like I'll get much help from Mr Cartwright, yonder.'

Patrick was beginning to lose patience with the young man. They'd all lost someone dear to them, but life went on. It had to.

'Okay, Patrick. Wish us luck!' Ben said.

Within seconds, Ben and Joe disappeared. The blanket of night had descended and covered everything outside a four-foot circle of the campfire.

'I'll leave you ladies to clear away,' Patrick said. 'I need to be further out, the light from the fire makes it impossible to see anything.'

'Ah, sure,' Siobhan said. 'When it comes to clearing away, Patrick always has a good reason to be somewhere else, an' that's for sure.'

The two women laughed and Patrick walked off into the night.

*   *   *

'It sure is dark, Pa,' Joe said to his father as they began a gradual ascent. Their eyes weren't used to the dark yet.

'It'll get better, son,' Ben said. 'Your eyes will become used to the dark. Look,' Ben pointed, 'the moon's coming out.'

As Joe raised his eyes the moon appeared from behind a dark cloud and immediately its silvery light painted the terrain.

Ahead, the blackness was impenetrable as the mountain peaks loomed in the distance. Their black, jagged peaks, some reflecting the moonlight off what they presumed was snow, stood sentinel to the new land they sought.

As they slowly walked on, Ben and Joe kept their eyes peeled. They really had no idea what, if anything, inhabited the land. To break the silence, Ben showed Joe how to load the .45s into the Winchester and explained the lever-action.

'You've got a sight right at the end of the barrel,' Ben said. 'And if you line that up with the one nearest you, you stand a fair chance of hitting what you're aiming at. But remember, if it's moving, to shoot slightly ahead. Practice will improve. If we get time before we reach California, maybe we can do some target shooting with the Colt's as well.

'That'd be *real* good,' Joe said, the enthusiasm obvious in his voice.

'Another thing I was told,' Ben continued. 'Hold your breath as you squeeze the trigger. Never pull at the trigger, just squeeze it nice an' easy. With your breath held, you won't shake so much.'

Joe nodded, taking it all in.

'Are Winchesters the best rifle, Pa?' the boy

asked. 'I ain't heard of no others.'

'Maybe they are, maybe they ain't,' Ben said. 'I don't know. I looked at Remington and a Henry rifle in the store, but these Winchesters are new. So I guess they might be.'

Their conversation was halted abruptly by a howling that seemed to be all around them. Joe froze, his knuckles turned white as he gripped the rifle.

The howling continued, other howls joined in until a great cacophony of sound reverberated off the rocks.

'Coyotes, probably,' Ben said. 'That's the first time I've heard that noise. Or maybe wolves,' he added. He didn't know which; either way, they were a threat.

Father and son remained stock-still, their eyes moving like bullets from side to side in the half-light, waiting to see if they could detect movement.

A roar split the air, close by. The howling stopped. They heard snorting and heavy footfalls.

'What d'you think that is, Pa?' Joe whispered.

'Damned if I know,' Ben replied, and he loaded a slug into the chamber of his rifle.

Without saying another word, Joe did likewise. The two stood and waited, hardly daring to breath.

The roar sounded out again, the howling from the coyotes had ceased. There were grunts and sniffs and scratchings, but neither of them could see anything moving.

A roar that was so close it was almost deafening made both men jump. Then they heard the sound of a whimpering animal and then the sound of paws and claws scraping on rock. The noises receded, and they could hear slurping and crunching.

Then silence returned.

They waited a few more minutes, just to make sure the danger had passed, then Ben tapped his son on the shoulder and pointed forwards.

The resumed their hunt, treading as lightly as they could. Ben put his fingers to his lips, indicating to his son not to speak. Although the night air was full of small sounds, Ben was making sure that whatever had roared had gone someplace else.

Just when he thought it was safe, a huge, pitch-black object seemed to rise out of the very rock.

The head, which Joe thought was at least twenty-feet off the ground, was enormous. Either side of the giant head were arms, raised, that seemed to be as thick as tree-trunks and just as long.

Neither Joe not Ben said a word. It was as if they were mesmerized by the sudden appearance of such a monster.

'Oh my God,' Ben whispered, 'it must be a bear!'

As he spoke, a roar escaped the huge animal's snarling mouth, light reflecting off the long, sharp teeth. Joe was sure he could feel the animal's breath on his face as it roared like the very devil himself.

The bear readied itself to attack.

'Run, Joe, run,' Ben yelled at his son and loosed

off a shot and fought with the lever-action to load another slug into the chamber.

The slug missed its enormous target, thudding harmlessly into the ground, and the giant beast lunged forward. Ben could see blood and saliva dripping from its massive mouth.

Joe, who'd not thought to question his father, but did as he was told, stopped when he heard the shot. He had hoped to see the body of the animal dead. What he saw was his father struggling with the lever-action on the Winchester. As he watched, his father, who was pacing backwards away from the bear, fell. The rifle exploded as he dropped it, and the bullet flew into the air.

Without thinking, Joe raised his rifle, placing the stock slowly, deliberately, into his right shoulder.

Although the night air was cold, he could feel sweat beading on his forehead. Carefully, he sighted down the long barrel, aligning both sights.

The eyes of the huge beast, although more intent on the fallen man, seemed to stare back at Joe in a blank, dead, glassy stare that said I'm coming after you next!

Taking a deep breath, Joe remembered what his father had told him no more than five minutes' before.

His finger, resting on the trigger, felt wet and slippery as he began to squeeze the cold metal towards him.

The flash and the explosion as the slug left the barrel threw Joe off guard. It was the first time he'd fired a gun of any description, and the power was a tad more than he'd expected.

The bear, poised over the prone body of his father, had time to raise its head just as the bullet slammed into his left eye.

A roar that had started a split second before the slug hit, was cut short.

The huge frame of the bear sank slowly to the ground and its deadly jaws now harmless, landed on Ben Dowie's legs.

Joe, temporarily blinded by the muzzle flash, didn't know whether he'd hit the animal or not. He pulled the lever-action down and pushed it back up, ready to fire again.

But the bear had disappeared.

Panic almost set in as he thought the giant creature might have taken his father with him.

Joe walked forward, the love of his father overcoming the fear of the bear.

'Pa?' he called out tentatively, not knowing whether he'd get a reply or not.

Ben Dowie got himself up on one elbow and stared into the lifeless eye of the huge bear. Its coat, thick and brown, was stained red round the jaws where he'd obviously just finished his last meal. The lone black eye stared back him, the other was non-existent. For a second, Ben was reminded of the dog he'd had as a boy, the eye looked so peaceful and gentle.

But the teeth, razor-sharp and long, were designed to tear flesh from bone. The body, muscle-packed with enormous strength bore little relation to his old mutt.

'Joe,' Ben called out.

'Pa! You're alive.'

'Thanks to you, son,' Ben said, and wriggled his legs out from under the dead-weight of the bear.

Joe gently placed his rifle on the ground and flung his arms round his father's neck. He wasn't too old for that, or for the tears that ran down his face in relief.

*   *   *

The three men were easily catching up the lone rider. The sand muffled their horses' hooves and Eileen had no idea she was being followed.

From her right, she could hear the nearby lowing of the cattle as they plodded their way east. Every now and then a high-pitched whistle from the drovers or a whoop, to get would-be strays back in the herd, floated over the rise.

She heard one man calling out to another. She couldn't make out what was being said, but the voices were somehow comforting to hear.

The sounds caused her to smile. Her long auburn hair, glistening in the sunlight, was spread across her shoulders, her deep-blue eyes, alive with anticipation, her ruby-red lips, slightly parted in her smile, revealed teeth whiter than white.

The first she knew about the men following her was when her bridle was roughly grabbed and a leather-clad hand swiped her across the face.

The last thing Eileen remembered was the sand rushing up to meet her as she was knocked off her horse.

SEVEN

The fall badly winded Eileen. She felt as if a great weight had been placed on her chest, compressing it, making breathing almost impossible. Gradually, it became easier and she felt less dizzy.

She had no time to recover fully. She heard cows in the distance, the calls of the drovers, and, nearby, she heard the sound of men landing in the sand beside her head.

Before she had time to look up, a black sack, rough and smelly, was pulled over her face. Darkness descended.

Pull strings were tightened round her neck and her arms were roughly pulled behind her and bound. Although her breathing was coming easier by the minute, the air inside the black sack became fetid. Whatever had been kept in the sack had gone bad a long time ago. She began to gag as the air inside her hood heated up and the smell became more than she could bear.

Eileen blacked out.

Two men manhandled her back into her saddle, grabbing the reins so that the horse couldn't escape, and while one mounted, the other handed him Eileen's reins.

It was all over in a matter of seconds and none of the men had uttered a word.

Turning now, they headed back in the direction from which they'd come, towing Eileen's mount between them.

Keeping a close look at the top of the deserted rise to their left, the three men breathed a collective sigh of relief: everything had gone exactly as they'd planned it.

The ride back to the cabin would take thirty minutes, another ten to make sure the girl was secure, and the three would be out checking fences before two and nobody would be any the wiser.

They left the desert, its perimeter marked at first by a few small cactus plants, then larger ones. Stunted trees and a whisper of grass that looked green from a distance but as soon as you rode through it, it was so sparse it wouldn't hide a flea.

The ground became firmer, the grass thicker and, in a matter of a quarter of a mile, the four horses picked their way through prairie land; the sandy soil changed colour and consistency the nearer they got to the riverbed.

There was a sweet smell in the air, despite the heat of the early afternoon, that rose up from the fertile earth. The horses cantered with more willingness as they caught the smells of water, fertile soil and lush grass.

The four riders reached the blind canyon without mishap. They'd fully expected to see or be seen by someone and they were ready to kill as needs be in order to maintain secrecy.

Eileen Malloy regained consciousness as her mount came to a halt. The fetid air inside the hood was just as she'd remembered it, but it took her a while to comprehend what was going on.

She'd been abducted. That much she was sure of. But by whom? And why?

She felt hands roughly grab her round the waist and drag her to the ground. Her legs felt weak and she knew that, but for the arms holding her upright, she'd fall over.

She was standing in sand, it was soft so she could tell, and, as she tried to get her wits about her, she was marched forwards. The small step leading into the abandoned cabin caught her right foot and Eileen staggered, her full weight being taken by the two pairs of hands that held her. She felt something hard underfoot and knew she was being taken inside somewhere, but for the life of her she couldn't think of where that was likely to be.

She was disorientated. Not just because of the black sacking over her head – that was bad enough – but she'd no idea how long she'd been unconscious. They could have been riding for half a day or half an hour.

The sounds changed now, as well; her footfalls were slightly muffled, so she knew she was inside somewhere. A creaky door was opened and she felt cool air on her hands. Then she was led forwards – and down.

The temperature dropped dramatically as, led in the front and rear, Eileen was taken down a flight of rickety wooden steps. Terror and horror filled her mind. She was being led underground!

* * *

'You saved my life, son,' Ben said with awe in his voice. He'd realized a few weeks back that his boy was a boy no longer, that their relationship had altered now. Ben was addressing an equal, he was talking to someone who'd saved his life for certain.

'It weren't nothin', Pa,' Joe said, feeling embarrassed more than anything else.

'Maybe nothin' to you,' Ben said, 'but I value my life.' Ben grinned at his son and got to his feet.

'Gee, Pa,' was all Joe could think of to say.

Seeing that his son was embarrassed, Ben changed tack. 'Reckon there's enough meat on this ole grizzly to keep us fed 'til we reach Califonia.'

'You mean you can eat bear?' Joe asked.

'Reckon so. It's an animal, ain't it? Heard stories of people eating snakes and skunks and most anything else, so I figure bear is eatable.'

Father and son stood looking down at the huge frame of the dead bear. Suddenly, Joe felt a wave of guilt as he realized the enormity of taking a life.

'Was it right, Pa,' he said. 'Killing the bear, I mean?'

'Well, killin' anythin' is a matter for your con-science, son,' Ben said, weighing his words care-fully. 'What you gotta remember is, by killin' this bear, you saved me from certain death an', at the same time, you've provided fresh meat. Nothin' will go to waste.' Ben smiled down at his son.

'I guess,' Joe said, but he didn't sound all that convinced at that time.

'Well, unless you got hidden strengths that I don't know about,' Ben said, 'I reckon we get this critter skinned and the meat stored afore the wolves or whatever come sniffin' around.'

Ben and Joe worked quickly. Neither had skin-ned an animal of any description before, but they soon got the hang of it, even though they'd slit the bear along its back instead of its belly.

'You cart some of this back to the camp,' Ben said, 'an' I'll keep cuttin'. If we both go, by the time we get back there'll be nothin' left.'

'Okay, Pa,' Joe said and loaded up with the still steaming meat.

It took nearly an hour to transport all the meat Ben thought they'd need. The entrails, steaming and stinking, they left with the skeleton. Unknown to them, the woods surrounding them were filled with eyes, watching and waiting.

Ben was amazed when he returned to the campsite to learn that Joe had not said a word about what had happened. Martha was beside herself with worry – something Joe and Ben couldn't understand as the danger was now long past.

Late as it was, Martha, Eileen and Siobhan began to rub salt into the meat. They left two large hunks unsalted as they felt sure they'd use it before it had time to go bad on them.

Joe stuck a steak of bear meat on a stick and held it in the flames of the campfire. He wasn't hungry, but he needed to find out what it tasted like, first. It was his kill, and for all they knew, the meat would taste terrible.

It didn't. A bit chewy, but anyone would have been hard-pushed to say just exactly *what* meat they were eating. Joe passed the steak round so that everyone could sample it.

'See,' Ben said, 'just as good as beef – almost.'

Everyone laughed, and for the first time in a few weeks, they retired for the night feeling optimistic about their new lives.

From behind them, through the dark night air, came rending sounds and growls as Mother Nature took care of what remained of the bear.

*   *   *

Martin O'Flynn was not normally a cautious man. He'd worked for Patrick Malloy for nearly seven years now. First as a hand, then foreman, until now he was almost a part of the Malloy household.

There was something he didn't like about the three men Patrick had hired. They were too amenable, for one thing. No one, and that included Martin, *volunteered* to ride the fences. It was too hot, there was no shelter and you could be away from a decent bed and food for days on end.

They must have had an ulterior motive, he'd thought to himself. And no matter how many times he tried to push these doubts to the back of his mind, they always came bouncing back again.

As the thoughts wouldn't go away, O'Flynn decided he'd do a little detective work himself. It had been a few weeks now since he'd been out in the saddle and, although not all that keen on the idea, he knew he wouldn't rest until he'd put his mind at ease.

Telling his second-in-command, as he called him, Stu Firks, that he needed to get away for a day or two, he stocked up with a sleeping roll, some vittals and mounted up.

'How long you gonna be, boss?' Stu asked.

'Long as it takes,' O'Flynn replied and wheeled his horse round and set off at a steady gallop.

* * *

Eileen sat tied to a centre pole in the middle or the root cellar. The ground was hard on her backside and cold. As she sat, tears rolled down her face at the utter frustration of not knowing who or why she'd been taken like this.

The cords that bound her arms and wrists were already digging into her soft flesh and although she couldn't see, she knew they were bleeding.

Soft, scurrying sounds filled her head as she imagined rats or mice or worse running about the dank cellar.

Above, she could hear the footfalls of the men who'd kidnapped her. She could hear muffled voices, laughter, but she couldn't hear what was being said.

A door slammed closed and silence fell like a cloak. Eileen Malloy felt that she'd never been so alone in her life.

She vaguely remembered hearing horses galloping before she blacked out again.

*   *   *

The three cowboys slowed their mounts down about half-an-hour later. They'd reached the fence, again without being seen, five miles out from the ranch-house. Not a great distance, but they'd allowed for that.

They'd covered their tracks pretty well. The day before, two of the men had ridden the fence-line and made running repairs just before dusk. Anyone who'd followed the fence today would see freshly-stamped out soil and so would assume they were doing their job.

Lighting up a cigarette and relaxing for the first time that day, the three allowed their animals to walk at their own pace.

Tomorrow, they'd put the second part of the plan into action: the ransom.

Ten long years in the penitentiary had taught them a lot. Patience, especially. Vengeance was one thing, but money did a body a whole lot better.

Turning, they saw the lone figure approaching

at a canter.

'Didn't take him long,' the leader of the three said under his breath.

'Howdy, boys,' O'Flynn called out.

'Boss,' came a muttered reply. 'What brings you out?'

'Oh, I get out now and then, get the softness out of me head and the fresh air into me lungs. Saw you've already done some repairs,' O'Flynn said eyeing each of the men in turn.

'Sure. That's what we's supposed to be doin',' the same man replied.

A silence fell, O'Flynn was racking his brain for conversation but it was obvious the three hands were not. After a couple of minutes, O'Flynn bid them farewell and galloped on ahead of them. He still felt uneasy, and for the life of him he couldn't understand it. Sure, they hadn't got far, but then he'd seen the evidence of their work that morning. Maybe they were just slow, he reasoned. He was tempted to turn and look back, but he resisted it. He felt they suspected him of something already. So he just rode on. He'd wait ahead at a place he knew he couldn't be seen and just watch. That was all he could do.

'We're gonna have to git rid of him,' the leader said in a matter-of-fact tone. 'I reckon he's on to us.'

'How can he be?'

'I don't know, but somethin's botherin' the hell out of our Mr O'Flynn.'

'Goddamn, look, one o' the posts is bust.'

The three reined in and dismounted.

'Git a fire goin', I could sure use a coffee.' The leader grabbed a hold of a fence post and flung it to the ground.

They were equipped with four each, tied to the rear of their saddle. If they needed any more than that on their tour of inspection, they'd have to cut fresh ones, and they weren't too keen on that idea.

The tool bag was hanging from one side of the saddle's pommel, on the other, a bag of nails.

One of the other horses was carrying spare fence-wire, just a small coil in case wires got bust.

The fences were constantly under attack from wayward steers that'd just bounce into them as they fed sometimes. Wild animals could also prove a nuisance.

The fire lit, one of the gang sat, lit another cigarette and, reaching into his vest pocket, he pulled out a short piece of brown leather that was rough and broken at either end.

He rubbed it with his finger and thumb, feeling the smoothness on one side and the roughness on the other. It was part of a restraining strap for a saddle, and the man had kept it safe for ten years.

The other two began digging out the broken post. When it was free, they tossed it aside and joined the third man, who began pouring out coffee.

'Where'd you reckon he's off to?'

'I don't know. Where ever he's goin', I don't 'xpect to see him agen, leastways, not alive!'

The man replaced the leather strap in his vest

pocket and stood. He took a mouthful of coffee and threw the rest onto the ground, the soil sucked it up greedily and sun took care of the damp patch in less than a minute.

'Reckon I'll take me a short ride ahead,' he said. 'Might do a bit o' huntin'.'

'You take care, 'xpect some o' them critters can shoot back.' The three laughed with the laughter of men who were full of confidence.

EIGHT

Ben Dowie pulled hard on both reins and the brake handle, causing the wagon's wheels to skid to a halt in the sandy ground. A plume of fine dust rose into the air and Patrick Malloy, driving the second wagon, thanked him in no uncertain manner under his breath.

Ben stood on the running board and threw his hat high into the air.

'Yahooo!' he screamed at the top of his voice.

'Is the man having a fit?' Patrick called. From his position, he couldn't see what Ben was looking at.

'Patrick Malloy,' Ben called out, his voice sounding manic and high-pitched. 'Come down here and feast your Irish eyes on this!'

Patrick jumped from the wagon and ran forwards. Ben all but dragged him up onto the front of his wagon. 'Feast your eyes,' Ben yelled.

Patrick shook his head in disbelief. Below them, no more than a day's journey, two at the outside, lay the promised land. The virgin land that already, blood had been shed for. They'd risked everything to get this far and now, there it was.

Patrick's excitement was tempered. 'How do you know that's our land?' he asked.

Ben didn't say a word. He brought out the Government map and showed Patrick the two shaded areas. 'Look,' he said. 'The river running north–south, the mountains and there, look, the pass!'

Patrick studied the map, looked down into the plain, and then back at the map. His hat flew even higher than Ben's had.

'We did it, be-Jesus!' he shouted at the heavens, 'we did it!'

The two men hugged and then jumped to the ground. Already, from the backs of both wagons, their families were alighting, trying to see what all the noise was about.

'Martha,' Ben called, 'there it is!' He picked his wife up as if she were a feather and squeezed her so tight she feared he'd break her ribs.

Patrick clung to Siobhan and openly wept.

Ben released his wife and a sombre atmosphere bore down on the small group: Ben, his wife Martha and son Joe, Patrick and Siobhan, with their children Pat junior and Eileen, and the lonely, bewildered figure of Doug Cartwright.

Ben lowered his head and gave thanks for their delivery, adding, 'I wish, good Lord, that the rest of our family and our departed friends, could be here this day.'

They stayed silent in prayer for a few moments, before Ben broke the mood.

'We'll camp here tonight,' he said. 'Tomorrow, we head down into that glorious valley!'

That night, Patrick brought out a little something that he'd kept well hidden and safe for the entire journey: a bottle of genuine Irish whiskey. It didn't take the three men long to devour its contents while Martha and Siobhan, aided by Eileen, roasted some more of the bear meat.

'Joe,' Ben called out to his son. 'There's enough left in this bottle for a final mouthful, and, with your permission, Patrick, I'd like Joe to have it.'

'Permission granted,' Patrick said with a grin that was not unaided by the potent spirit.

Joe stepped forward and took the bottle from his father. He'd never tasted beer before, let alone whiskey, but he felt a closeness to his father that he'd never felt before. Taking hold of the bottle in his right hand, he lifted it to his lips and in one swallow, downed the light-brown liquid.

He'd no sooner swallowed it than he was consumed in a fit of coughing that fair took the flesh off the back of his throat as the fiery liquid burned its way down to his empty stomach.

'First one's always the same,' Ben laughed and slapped his son on the back.

*   *   *

Now, ten years later, Ben Dowie stood atop the same rise, looking down into the valley that he'd turned into a successful ranch. Smoke curled lazily from his ranch-house and, in the distance, he could make out the home of his best friend, Patrick Malloy.

Ben liked to ride out to the rise and camp over at least once every month or so. He found it kept his head out of the clouds and did him good to recall the horrendous journey that had brought them to California.

The images were etched in his brain but visiting the site where they'd seen their own land for the first time also helped him to remember *never* to take anything for granted.

In the early days, work had filled all the daylight hours that God had seen fit to send. It was backbreaking work, not only on his spread but on Patrick's as well.

They must have shifted over a thousand tons of rock from the valley floor, doubtless an accummulation over the years when the river that gave life to all, was bigger and wider.

The rock had been put to good use. The two houses had taken nearly eighteen months to complete and eighty per cent of them was rock, hand-cut and each stone lovingly placed in postion. Even today, Ben could touch one of those same rocks on the house and remember the day it was put there.

This was the best time of the day as far as he was concerned. The sun was beginning to set way over to the west. The mountains that formed a backdrop to the valley, changed colour constantly, from grey to brown to purple and back again, finally turning as black as soot as the sun dipped behind their peaks.

A shadow loomed and spread across the valley almost duplicating the ragged horizon. Then, when the sun itself had finally disappeared, a red haze lit up the mountain tops. A deep red at the bottom, changing colour the higher up it went, finishing up black, to match the mountains themselves.

The blackness crept lower and lower until there was nothing to differentiate sky from land. Then the silvery rays of the moon added their brush-strokes to the constantly altering picture set out below him.

In the early days, Martha used to accompany him sometimes and Ben had sent for a tent through one of the catalogues that arrived periodically. Lately, Martha had declined his invitation more frequently, but always urging him to go when the mood took him.

She supplied him with food and Ben *always* took a bottle of Irish whiskey with him, although he only ever had two fingers-worth. He first toasted the health of the living, then those of absent friends and family that hadn't been fortunate enough to enjoy this land.

Ben set about lighting a fire. He always left it until it was pitch black because he found the brightness of the flames destroyed the sunset.

He followed the same ritual. The toasts, the fire, coffee and food, then he'd sleep under the stars; the tent was only for Martha's benefit.

Tonight was different. As he poured coffee, he was disturbed by the sound of approaching hooves.

Instantly, Ben was on his guard. The same Winchester he'd bought in Boston was by his side and in one swift movement, he'd picked it up and loaded it – ready.

'Ben? That you?' the Irish accent was unmistakable.

'Patrick?' Ben replied.

The rider and horse came into view. 'Martha said you'd be up here,' Patrick said.

'Nice to have company,' Ben said and reached for the whiskey bottle.

'Eileen's disappeared, Ben,' Patrick said without preamble.

Ben put the bottle back in his saddlebag and stood. 'How long's she been missing?'

'She went riding this morning and hasn't been seen since,' Patrick replied.

'You any idea where she went?'

'None. My stable lad's disappeared too.'

'You don't think they've …'

'Holy Mary mother of Jesus, no!' Patrick said emphatically. 'There's only one person in Eileen's life, as you well know.' To top it all, O'Flynn decided to go walk-about as well. And *he* hasn't returned.'

'You don't think it's just a coincidence?' Patrick asked.

'No, Ben. I wish I could think that. But I fear the worst.'

Ben thought for a while, then, 'Right. Let's get back. I'll send a couple of the boys to the herd. That should take them six seven hours if they push the horses. Let's make sure she hasn't gone out to join Joe. I'll give them orders to replace two drovers who can then gallop back here. It'll be a long night, Patrick, but there's little else we can do 'til daybreak.

Ben kicked sand and poured the coffee over the campfire and gathered his meagre possessions together. In less than three minutes, he was atop his horse and the two men began picking their way down the slope and back to Broken Saddle.

* * *

Martin O'Flynn rode on for another half hour before reining in and taking a breather.

Not much of a smoker, he preferred a cigar to pipe or cigarette, and he only smoked a cigar after dinner. Habits of a lifetime were there to be broken, and O'Flynn decided that today he *needed* a cigar.

The place he'd chosen to hide out in was only a hundred yards to his left off the trail. The land belonged not to Patrick Malloy, but to his friend, Ben Dowie. O'Flynn reckoned that Ben wouldn't mind a bit of trespassing – as long as it was in a good cause.

He unwrapped a cigar and stuck it between his teeth and, digging his spurs in, urged his mount forward at a walking pace. The comfort of merely having the cigar in his mouth delayed his actually lighting it until he'd found a gap in the fence to cross through.

Excellent, he thought, a broken fence as well. That meant that if the men *were* doing their job, they'd have to stop here anyway.

O'Flynn rode on to the outcrop and dismounted. He led his horse behind a huge boulder and tethered it with a rock, dropping oats on the ground from a bag slung behind his saddle. The animal chewed contentedly as O'Flynn made his way back out front.

Finding a comfortable spot and one that gave him an uninterrupted view down the fence line, O'Flynn struck a match on the boulder and puffed happily.

After the first hour had passed uneventfully, O'Flynn was beginning to doubt the three men would ever show up. He thought about another cigar, but one was quite enough for now. He was just going to check up on his horse, more through boredom than concern, when he spotted a distant rider. One man, not three, he thought.

'Damn an' hell!' O'Flynn mouthed audibly. He'd forgotten to bring a spy-glass so he'd have to wait until the rider was closer to see who it was.

The horseman seemed in no rush, his animal walked almost lazily along and O'Flynn could see smoke rising into the still air as the man exhaled. A small pall of dust hung around the ground behind him for a while, but sunk listlessly back to earth as he passed.

Straining his eyes in the bright sunlight, O'Flynn tried to ignore the heat-haze, the shimmer that rose up from the ground, and the sweat that was running down his back and seemed to be filling his boots.

Most of the approaching rider's face was in shadow, the broad brim of a dust-yellowed stetson was pulled way down low. O'Flynn wasn't sure, but it looked like one of the three strangers, if only he could get a better view.

Then it dawned on O'Flynn why the man seemed in no hurry. He looked again at the rider and it hit him like a .45 at close range.

He wasn't following the fence line, he was following O'Flynn's tracks!

NINE

In the black dankness of the root-cellar, Eileen Malloy regained consciousness.

She was cold and shivery and every bone in her body ached. She still had the black sacking over her head and for a moment, panic returned, then she remembered what had happened to her and fought to get her self-control back.

Breathing deeply – as deeply as the sacking would allow, for every time she inhaled through her mouth, the sacking closed in. She could feel her heart thudding away in her chest, her ears throbbed with its incessant beat. Gradually, the beating slowed down and she began to feel the icy cold sweat on her face followed by the soreness of her wrists and ankles where the ropes burned.

Her fingers were numb, she'd been slumped up against a floor post set in the middle of the cellar, and the ropes, combined with her body-weight, had hampered circulation to her hands.

Pulling herself together, she sat upright, feeling a sharp pain in her head and lower back. Slowly, she began moving her fingers up and down, trying to get blood and feeling back to them.

Logically, Eileen tried to figure out what was going on. That she'd been kidnapped was obviously beyond doubt. But why?

Her father was comfortable rather than wealthy, so any ransom would be difficult to meet. She hadn't seen any of her abductors, the only thing she remembered was the smell. One thing was certain, the men who'd captured her hadn't taken a bath in a long time.

Resting from the seemingly small exertion of wriggling her fingers, Eileen began again, this time moving the whole of her hands. The pain from her wrists was excruciating, but she knew that unless she got feeling back into her fingers she could be in serious trouble.

Blood, but it could have been sweat, ran down the palms of her hands in a steady, slow, rivulet that her imagination magnified.

The feeling of panic returned and no matter how hard she tried not to, Eileen began to cry with sheer frustration – as well as an overwhelming sense of hopelessness. She felt she was about to die.

*   *   *

The two riders reached the herd in just under three hours. It took another twenty minutes to locate Joe Dowie and realize the seriousness of Eileen's disappearance.

'How long has she been missing?' Joe asked. A

glazed look stared at the two Broken Saddle men.

'As far as we know, since this mornin',' one of the men replied.

'Young Jody's gone, too,' the other man added.

'Jody?' Joe repeated.

'He ain't bin seen, neither. Mr Dowie sent us out here jus' to make sure Miss Eileen ain't come out after you.'

'Hank,' Joe called out. 'I gotta get back.'

'Okay by me, Joe,' Hank said. 'You need any help?'

'No. There's enough men back there if needs be.'

Joe all but ran to his horse and leapt into the saddle. 'Come on,' he called to the two riders, 'let's go.'

Without waiting for a response or reply, Joe dug his spurs in and galloped back towards Broken Saddle.

'You boys better take fresh mounts,' Hank said. 'Them two ponies look all in.'

'Thanks, Hank.'

The two ranch-hands began unstrapping their saddles, while Hank organized replacements. Within five minutes, they were hot on the trail of Joe.

Joe looked neither left nor right. He rode in a blind panic. The tears in his eyes, part caused by the speed of his ride and part caused by the fear for Eileen's life, he blinked away.

Clearing the rear of the herd, ignoring the men who waved in greeting, the air became chokingly heavy with dust from the drive.

Without thinking, he steered his horse up the gentle slope that ran alongside the trail, aiming to get clearer air.

The horse slowed as its hooves dug into the comparatively soft sand of the slope and even after only five minutes' galloping, the animal's mouth began to foam and flecks flew back landing on Joe's chaps. Heedless of what he was doing to the animal in his blind panic, Joe dug his spurs in harder, forcing the animal into a pace he wouldn't be able to maintain.

Reaching the crest of the slope, the animal needed a rest, but Joe forced it on, using the rein as a whip and yelling all the time. The animal's ears were flat on its head and the whites of its eyes showed up in unexpected fear.

The two cowboys following Joe had taken to the slope from the off and their animals were in better condition. They were about two hundred yards behind Joe when they saw his horse crash to the ground.

They reached the stricken rider within two minutes. The horse was lying on its side, panting heavily. Joe, his right leg pinned beneath the horse, was conscious.

The two cowboys leapt from their animals and managed to get Joe's horse upright and, while one held on to the reins, the other attended Joe.

'Can you move your foot?' he asked Joe.

Joe nodded as he swivelled his ankle.

'Well, leastways it ain't broke,' the cowboy said. 'If 'n you don't mind me sayin',' the man went on, 'that sure was a damn fool way to ride a horse.'

Joe could only nod in agreement: 'I didn't think,' was all he said.

'Yeah, well, you ain't gonna do Miss Eileen no good all busted up,' the man said helping Joe to his feet.

'You're right, of course,' Joe said, his face reddening with embarrassment. 'I'll water the horse and take it easy.'

Remounted, the three men cantered back towards Broken Saddle.

* * *

O'Flynn was holding his breath. He couldn't get to his horse without the approaching rider seeing him and he sure couldn't stay where he was, unless he was prepared for a shoot-out. It had been a while since O'Flynn had faced another man with a gun ready to draw.

The rider stopped. For the first time he raised his head, looking first at the outcrop from top to bottom; then he followed the tracks that went alongside the fence.

O'Flynn recognized the face instantly, it was the one they called Dan Stacey. Now what the hell was he tracking me for? thought O'Flynn, keeping his head as low as he could and still be able to see. He daren't move his head as, although his stetson was almost the same colour as the boulder, he knew any movement no matter how slight, would give his position away.

The rider dismounted and knelt down by the side of his horse, studying the hoof marks. Even from this distance, O'Flynn could tell the man was a mite agitated and more wary than he had been on his approach.

As he watched, Stacey stood and slowly removed a rifle from the long scabbard fixed to the side of his saddle.

O'Flynn's horse whinnied.

For a second, it sounded like a clap of thunder in O'Flynn's ears and Stacey, who'd obviously heard the sound, pulled down the lever-action on the rifle and went down on one knee, the rifle rammed home against his right shoulder in one easy, well-practised movement.

O'Flynn, keeping his head steadier than a rock, slowly drew his faithful old .44 single action Remington Beals Army Revolver. The weapon felt heavy and comfortable in his hand as he brought his thumb up to cock the hammer. Although Stacey would have more accuracy from this distance, the handgun gave O'Flynn confidence enough that if push came to shove, he'd go down fighting.

Stacey scanned the area in minute detail, watching for anything that moved. He saw nothing. Staying low on one knee, sighting down the barrel of his rifle, he swept from left to right without even blinking.

He stayed down, ready, for another two minutes. During that time O'Flynn prayed his horse remained silent. Even the shifting of metal shoes on rock seemed to echo like a cannon-shot.

The silence dragged on. O'Flynn became uncomfortably aware of the sweat that soaked through his long-johns and his shirt and vest. It ran like rivers from beneath his hat, forcing its way through his eyebrows and running into the corners of his eyes, where it stung and affected his vision. It didn't matter how often he tried to blink them clear, the salt-water kept on flowing.

The deadlock was broken momentarily by two other riders. Evidently, thought O'Flynn, they'd repaired the fence. Shit! that means they're gonna repair the busted fence that O'Flynn had crossed through. They were bound to see his trail!

It was bad enough one on one, now, it was three on one. The harsh sunlight reflected off the blued barrel of his handgun and, for the first time, O'Flynn noticed that hand wasn't as steady as it ought.

The two newcomers reined in as Stacey stood. O'Flynn heard murmurings, but couldn't make out what they were saying. He recognized the other two, now, as well: Luke Palmer and Harley Young.

The two dismounted and Stacey leant his rifle against the fence. They unloaded wire and nails and tools and set to fix up the busted fence in silence. All the while, one or other of the three cast his eyes about the terrain. The one good thing, thought O'Flynn, was their own tracks had obliterated his.

The fence repair took fifteen, long minutes and

O'Flynn breathed a sigh of relief when they started to pack up their gear. Stacey mounted up and set to walking forwards, but the other two returned at a canter in the direction from which they'd come.

Where the hell they going? O'Flynn asked himself.

It didn't take Stacey long to discover that the tracks had ceased to exist. He circled around for a while but found nothing. Then he rode back to the newly repaired fence and scanned the ground on the other side.

O'Flynn saw the grin from where he crouched.

Stacey wheeled round and set off after his partners. He didn't glance back once.

*   *   *

Joe Dowie and the two ranch-hands reached Broken Saddle in record time, even though they hadn't pushed the animals. The two cowboys took care of the animals and Joe ran towards the house seeing his father and Patrick Malloy making towards him.

'You've answered one question,' Patrick said.

'Question?' Joe asked, flustered.

'We were hoping Eileen had gone to join you,' Ben replied.

'Still no news, then,' Joe said dejectedly.'

'No. Now we know where she *isn't*,' Patrick said, 'I'll round up my men and start a proper search.'

Ben glanced at the sky. The sun was way over to

the west and they all knew that in less than three hours night would fall whether they found Eileen or not.

If she was injured and lying out on the range somewhere, the three men tried not to think too much about the cold and wild animals, but the looks they exchanged conveyed that message clearly.

Patrick left for Blarney, while Joe ran to the bunkhouse and gathered half-a-dozen willing volunteers.

Ben walked across to the stable to get a fresh animal after asking Martha to maybe go and keep Siobhan company.

Martha readily agreed and Ben organized the buggy for her.

There was nothing more he could do now, except hope to God that Eileen was alive and that they found her before anything or anyone else.

TEN

A plan was drawn up: Ben Dowie was determined that the search shouldn't go off half-cocked, with riders out all over the range in a random pattern.

He gathered the men outside the main stable and, with the aid of a map he'd drawn up himself over the years, detailed what he thought was the best way of going about the search.

'I want you men to ride in twos,' he began. 'That way, you've all got backup.

'If – when you find her, I want three shots firing in quick succession. If Eileen is injured, then one rider stays with her and the other returns to Broken Saddle. Okay?'

The men nodded and grunted agreement.

'Now, pair off and form a queue and I'll allocate the search area so we don't double up and waste time searching the same place twice.'

The group of men did as they were told, and pair by pair, Ben sent them on their way.

As the men left, Patrick returned bringing six men with him. Ben quickly despatched them

'Patrick, I reckon you an' me an' Joe ride

together,' Ben said when the last pair had ridden off.

'Ah, be-Jesus, Ben. It's such a big country,' Patrick sighed.

'Patrick, if she's to be found, we'll find her. You have my word on that,' Ben said. 'Now come on, let's go.'

The two men mounted up. 'Maybe we'll find Jody and O'Flynn, as well,' Ben added as they set off.

'Aye, maybe,' Patrick said absently.

Martha was sitting atop the buggy and she'd dragged Doug Cartwright along as well. He hadn't been all that keen to leave Broken Saddle. In the ten years since they'd started the ranch, Doug had never set foot outside it.

'You keep an eye on Martha, Doug,' Ben called out as his wife set off.

Doug Cartwright nodded and waved his rifle in the air, but he didn't call back.

Ben watched as the buggy left carrying his wife to the Blarney Stone ranch.

'Seems like Doug's comin' out of his shell,' he said to Patrick.

'Well, he's stopped the booze. Maybe he'll pull himself together.'

'Maybe,' Ben said, but his voice betrayed doubt.

Leaving Broken Saddle behind them, the two riders and the buggy set off in a V, Martha heading north-west, Ben and Patrick north-east.

Ben had picked the hardest stretch of land to search: the foothills of the Sierra Nevada range.

He'd also picked it, because, like Patrick, he knew it was a favourite place of Eileen's. All three men had ridden the trails and paths there with her, camping out sometimes and admiring both sunset and sunrise as well as the magnificent view of both ranches in the valley below and the vast tract of desert that stretched to the eastern horizon and beyond.

While seeming relaxed, Ben and Patrick scanned the terrain, looking for the slightest signs of movement.

Then they saw the approaching, riderless horse.

* * *

As soon as Martin O'Flynn felt it was safe to get his horse, he holstered his Remington and left his hidey-hole.

The horse was non-plussed at his return, neither looking up or showing any signs of greeting. The oats O'Flynn had spread on the ground were all gone, but that didn't stop the animal from nuzzling the barren ground in expectation of finding more food.

O'Flynn grabbed the reins and mounted up. He steered the animal back towards the fence where he crossed over, but, of course, now that it was repaired he'd have to find another gap.

Heading first in the opposite direction, he stopped and thought that stupid. He wanted to see where the three riders were heading. They should have been riding the fence line north, now, they were heading back south. Why?

As foreman of the Blarney Stone, it was O'Flynn's job to check up on the itinerant drifters who came and went through the valley. The regular hands he could trust, he'd known them for a while, but the drifters?

He turned his horse south and set off at a walk. The fence-line stretched out in front of him bearing east as it skirted the foothills and disappeared.

O'Flynn was cautious. If the three *had* been tracking him, they could very well be lying in wait. Trouble was, there was no other avenue for him to follow. To the east, foothills, rocky land that even the wild critters would have difficulty negotiating let alone his horse. To the west, apart from the fence, was open range land with no cover.

As Martin O'Flynn was trying to make up his mind on a plan of action, three shots rang out in quick succession: the second one slammed into O'Flynn and sent him flying from the saddle, landing heavily in the dirt. His head slammed into a rock and Martin O'Flynn didn't move.

Dan Stacey grinned to himself. He knew the foreman was hiding out, but he didn't know where and he didn't have the time to waste looking for him.

It was, of course, Luke who'd suggested they ride back south and draw the man out. The plan had worked. Now they were free to do as they liked for a while.

Setting up camp, they didn't want to risk heading back to the cabin in daylight, Luke Palmer set about trying to write a ransom note.

He sat cross-legged on the ground, his tongue licking his lips in concentration as the stubby pencil scrawled out a simple message:

WE GOT THE GIRL
$10,000 WE'LL
LET YOU KNOW
WHEN.

Satisfied, Luke Palmer grunted, folded up the tattered piece of paper and wrote *Patrick Malloy* on the outside.

'Now, all we gotta do is git this to the house,' he said. 'Then we kin sit back an' wait fer the money.'

'We gonna let the girl go?' Harley asked.

'Hell no. An' eye fer an eye. Ain't that what you bin sayin' these past ten years?' Palmer said and then spat into the dirt.

'She didn't kill Slim,' Harley said.

'Maybe she didn't,' Luke replied, 'but she was with 'em.'

'I don't know why we don't jus' ride on in there and kill 'em all,' Stacey said.

'You numbskull,' Luke said with contempt. 'We do that an' where we gonna get our foldin' money?'

'We could rob 'em,' Stacey replied as if it was obvious.

'So you reckon a sheep-farmer's gonna have ten grand jus' lyin' about the house waitin' fer us to go rob it, huh? Shit fer brains.'

Stacey kept silent. He knew it was pointless arguing with Palmer, he always came off second best.

'You take care o' that nosey foreman?' Palmer asked.

'Sure did, he flew outta his saddle like a vulture on heat,' Stacey replied with a beaming grin on his face.

'He dead?'

'Well, if 'n he ain't, he sure soon will be!' Stacey flopped down beside the other two. The three men relaxed, waiting for the sun to go down.

'I don't reckon we should hole-up here too long,' Harley said after a couple of minutes' thought.

'Oh, you don't, do ya?' Palmer said. 'An' what reckonin' did you use to think that out all by yourself?'

'Stands to reason,' Harley replied, not being put off by Palmer's sarcasm. 'S'posin' somebody heard the shootin'? They might jus' come a-ridin' on out here and here we is, sittin' down as if we ain't got no cares in the world.'

Palmer was about to lambast Harley when he suddenly realized that the man made sense.

'Harley, there are times when even you can come up with a piece of reckoning that makes a deal of sense.'

Palmer stood, stretched his lean frame and ambled over to his horse.

'What now?' Stacey asked.

'Ain't you bin a-listenin'? Young Harley here's bin a-reckoning. Come on, let's move.'

* * *

The approaching horse stopped as it neared Ben, Patrick and Joe. Pawing the ground, the animal stood and waited for them to approach.

'You recognize it, Ben?' Patrick asked.

'Yeah, I recognize it. It belongs to Jody.'

'Your stablelad?'

'The very same,' Ben said and dismounted. He inspected the animal carefully, looking to see if it was injured or bore any clues as to the rider's whereabouts. But it was clean. No marks, no clues.

'Could've come in from anywheres,' Ben said.

'Look at the reins,' Joe said. 'They're hangin' loose over its head.'

'By God, you're right!' Ben said

'So what if they are?' Patrick asked.

'It means the rider got off and left the horse,' Joe said. 'Didn't fall, or get shot off. He left the horse parked up someplace.'

'Could be he was meetin' someone,' Ben added.

'You think that might've been Eileen?' Patrick asked.

Joe's face fell, fit to hit his boots.

'I doubt it,' Ben said. 'Jody's just a kid. Doesn't have much of a brain to write home about. Unless I'm badly mistaken, Eileen only had eyes for one person.' Ben turned to look at Joe.

'Ah, to be sure,' Patrick agreed. 'She's never looked at anyone else.'

Joe reddened under the smiling faces of the two men.

'Well, best we can try an' do,' Ben started, changing the subject to spare Joe's embarrassment, 'is to track this here animal, see where it leads us.'

'Makes sense to me,' Patrick intoned.

'Well, come on, let's get goin',' Joe said, his impatience beginning to show.

They remounted, taking the spare horse with them, and began to follow the tracks.

The horse had run a straight line, no meandering. It was probably on its way back to the Blarney Stone when they ran into it.

The three followed the trail for twenty minutes in complete silence. Each man concentrating on the job in hand. If they let their imaginations run riot, if they even thought to themselves that Eileen was badly hurt or worse, they might miss something of importance.

It was Joe who heard the shots. At first he wondered whether it was his imagination, as neither Ben nor Patrick seemed to show any signs of having heard them. They were distant, but he was sure he heard three shots, fired in quick succession. The signal each man had been told to use.

'You hear that, Pa?' he said.

'Hear what?' Ben asked.

'Three shots.'

'Nope.'

'I did,' Patrick said. 'Difficult to pin-point, but I think north-east of here.'

Without further ado, the three set to galloping in the direction they *hoped* the signal came from and meant that Eileen had been found.

ELEVEN

Patrick Malloy junior had missed out on all the excitement. Since sun-up that day he'd been out in his beloved fields, tending the crops that he saw as the life-blood of Blarney Farm.

Now, late afternoon, he was ready to go home. He loaded up the small wagon with his tools, took a mighty swig from the water barrel and, hands on hips, stared at the field of corn that was reaching maturity. The cobs swelling almost as he looked at them. It would be a fine harvest this year, he thought. What with the corn, the sheep and the potatoes, Blarney Farm would have more than enough food to survive the harsh winter, the surplus would be sold and the profit used for seed for next spring.

Contented that all was well at Blarney Farm, Pat junior climbed aboard the wagon and set off back to the house at a leisurely pace.

The air, although hot from the heat of the day, was clear and sweet to his nose. The irrigation channels that Pat had dug himself had done their job well. The soil was lush and black and, so far, he'd had little trouble with disease or pests. He knew that couldn't last, Mother Nature wasn't *that* bountiful all the time.

Pat's thoughts of his idyllic life were rudely interrupted by the sight of a horse drinking from one of the ditches. He couldn't see a rider, but the corn, standing in some places over five-feet tall, could hide anybody.

He steered the wagon towards the drinking animal and then he recognized it at once.

It was Eileen's pony.

Reining in and setting the brake, Pat stood and scanned the area.

'Eileen!' he yelled. 'Eileen, where are you?'

Silence greeted his calls. More silent now than it had been as his voice had every living creature in the vicinity on guard.

'Eileen, will you stop this messing about and come out.'

Still no reply, but Pat was unconcerned. His sister had always had a wicked sense of humour, so it didn't surprise him that she was hiding from him. She'd probably been lying in wait to trick him.

'I'm going, Eileen,' he called out. 'Sun'll be down soon and I'm tired and hungry.'

He sat and set the wagon in motion, looking all around him as the wagon trundled forwards, trying to find her hidey-hole.

His first sense of foreboding was when Eileen's horse began to follow the wagon.

'Eileen, your horse is following me. It's a long

walk home,' he called out, not looking round this time, sure that Eileen would pop up out of the field of corn.

She didn't.

Pat reined in the wagon again, Eileen's horse standing at the rear. 'Eileen, come out now, enough's enough.'

Pat strained his ears, thinking his sister might have fallen. He jumped from the wagon and, securing her pony to the tail-gate, he walked back to where he first saw the animal drinking.

He saw the hoof marks of the horse in the damp, black soil, but there were no signs of human prints, except his own.

He walked down a row of corn, studying the ground, looking for any sign; there were none, not a blade of corn broken, not a footprint. It was clear to him now that Eileen wasn't playing games. She just hadn't been here!

Pat ran back to the wagon and, releasing the brake, he urged the pair on, no more the leisurely pace. Something was wrong and he needed to get help as quickly as possible.

Reaching the farm, his sense of foreboding deepened. The place was all but deserted. Parked outside the house was the buggy he'd seen Martha drive so often.

Rushing inside, the gloom and despair hit him like a wall.

'What's happened?' Pat asked, dreading the answer.

It was Martha who replied, Siobhan sat staring

at the fireplace, her hands twisting in her lap. By the window stood Doug Cartwright. He was staring through the glass, sweeping the landscape, hoping he'd see Eileen riding home.

'Eileen's gone missing,' Martha said. 'Everyone's out searching, but so far no news.'

'I found her horse,' Pat said. 'It was out by the north field.'

Doug wheeled round. 'No sign of her?'

'No. I looked everywhere, I thought she was just teasing me,' Pat said.

'Come on,' Doug said with more authority than he had shown for years. 'We can't do nothin' here, let's go back to the cornfield and start from there.'

Siobhan still sat staring into the flames. She neither blinked nor seemed to hear what was being said.

'You two go,' Martha said, 'I'll take care of your mother.'

'Thanks, Martha,' Pat said and the two men left the house and ran across to the stable. They were lucky, there were three horses inside.

'I'll take care of Eileen's pony when we bring her home,' Pat said hopefully.

'And I'll help you,' added Doug.

The two men saddled up and galloped back to the cornfield. At least, Doug thought, they had a starting point.

*   *   *

Stacey, Palmer and Harley Young cut through the

foothills heading south. Stacey kept watch to the rear, while Harley stared ahead. Luke Palmer just rode, smoking, leaving the other two to do their business.

The sun was already making its daily slide into the western horizon as they rode over broken rock and shale, making a slight detour to get back to the cabin. Unknown to them, there were now over thirty men scouring the vicinity looking for Eileen Malloy.

None of the men had given her much thought while they'd been out, but Luke Palmer had already decided what the next part of the plan would be.

He'd send Harley to the farm with the ransom note. He figured they wouldn't harm him; if they did, they'd never see the girl again. As it was, Luke had made up his mind they never would.

The death of Slim Young all those years ago might have receded in the memory of his younger brother, Harley, but the chain of events that led them to the waystation and the run-in with Pat Garrett that resulted in ten years' hard labour in the state penetentiary, had built up in Palmer's mind to the extent that he could think of little else.

It had taken Palmer nearly four years to track down the families. Although in prison, he still had friends on the outside, people he'd dealt with over the years selling property he'd robbed.

The country was so big, they could have gone anywhere, but a chance remark in a gunshop had pinpointed their destination.

Unwittingly, the man who'd sold Ben Dowie his first rifle and pistol, had been responsible for their detection.

He'd used that sale to Dowie as a sales pitch ever since, and, four years later, was still using it. Unfortunately, the man he used it on that day in Boston, was a trader of dubious character and chief buyer from Palmer. Seeing a way of making a quick buck, he'd lost no time in telling Palmer of their whereabouts.

From then on, Palmer spent the next six years using his contacts to get their exact location.

When he was told the name of the ranch, a sinister grin spread across his face, as it did now while he thought about it. Broken Saddle.

The dang fool had even named his ranch after Slim's saddle.

Harley was looking at Luke strangely. He'd watched as *that* grin spread over Luke's face and knew what it meant; trouble.

'What you starin' at, boy?' Palmer spat at him.

'Nothin',' jus' lookin' is all,' Harley stammered.

'Well don't,' Palmer said. 'I don't take kindly to bein' stared at.'

'Sorry, Luke. I din't mean nothin' by it,' Harley apologized.

'Come sundown,' Palmer said, 'I want you to deliver this here ransom note to the farm.'

'Why me?' Harley complained.

'Why not? Slim *was* your brother, weren't he?'

'You know'd he was.'

'Then you take the note. An' I don't want you

a-lettin' no one follow you, neither,' Palmer said.

'Hell!' Harley exclaimed, 's'posin' they shoot me!'

'That ain't likely,' Palmer said coolly. 'Not if 'n they want to see the girl agen.'

Harley thought about that. It seemed to make sense, but he still had misgivings about showing his face at Blarney Farm.

* * *

The sun was dipping fast now and as Doug and Pat reached the cornfield, they realized that, in their haste to do something, they'd ignored the time of day.

Long fingers of black shadow began to claw their way through the swaying cornfields as the sun sank behind the distant mountains. Soon, the two men knew, any attempt at a search would be futile.

Out on the range and all around them, men rode in total concentration. The two families had strong ties and their workers were treated as part of those families, so the men felt they had lost one of their own.

Purely on a whim, two of the men had set off in the same direction as the cattle drive. They knew both Eileen and Joe, and they just couldn't get it out of their heads that Eileen had gone after him. What puzzled them, as it did everyone else, was what had happened to Jody?

Cresting the ridge, they saw the tracks left by

Joe and the other two hands. Further out, they saw another set of tracks.

Glancing wordlessly at each other, with sun going down fast, they made their way across the desert.

Something wasn't right with the tracks.

At first, they thought eight or nine riders had been out in the desert, but reached one of those weird areas in the desert where an underground stream passed by. Too deep to be of any use to a parched man, it nevertheless allowed small plants, with roots ten times as long as their height, to grow, binding the sand tight around themselves and making a firm area.

The tracks then told a different tale to the experienced cowpokes.

Three riding east but *four* riding west.

'Could be 'pokes from the drive,' one suggested.

'Don't make sense,' the other countered. 'If 'n they was from the drive, why're they heading back to Broken Saddle?'

'Maybe they were chasin' strays.'

Both men looked around the terrain: 'You see any sign o' cattle?'

'Nope.'

'Then there ain't bin no strays.'

'Lookee here,' the man pointed to the ground beneath them. 'Is my eyes a-deceivin', or was one o' them horses a pony? See, the tacks ain't so deep, an' the hooves are smaller compared to the others.'

'Hell, you're right. Could be Miss Eileen's, all

right. Come on, let's see where they lead us.'

As the sun dipped below the mountain skyline, the two cowboys walked their horses back towards Broken Saddle. The light was falling, fast, twilight was a bad time of the day. That's when the demons came out to play, tricks of the half-light that put the very devil up most folk.

Not only was the light getting fainter, the tracks were as well. The shifting sand had obliterated most, and in some places, all the indentations.

All they hoped for was that the odd patches of compacted sand wouldn't yield up the tracks as easy.

Within ten minutes, the two men had to dismount to peer through the gloom.

'We ain't gonna get much further tonight,' one said.

'Reckon you're right. Should we camp out, so's we don't lose our position, or get back?'

'I figure stayin' is better. We can be ready at first light.'

So the two men began gathering anything that would burn. Coffee being a priority, and then sleep.

* * *

Pat and Doug had reached the same conclusion. The light was gone now and, with no moon, the likelihood of stumbling across Eileen in the rows of corn would be like finding a needle in a haystack.

'Come on, Pat,' Doug said. 'Ain't no use ferretin' round here in the dark. We'll come back at first light. At least we got a start here.'

Reluctantly, Joe agreed. The two mounted up and headed back to the farm. Each hoping that maybe some of the others had had better luck than they'd had.

*   *   *

Ben, Patrick and Joe reached the foothills where Joe thought the shots had come from. Almost pitch black, they could hardly see more than five feet in any direction.

'Hush up,' Joe said.

They all remained stock still.

'There, you hear that?' Joe said.

Concentrating all their efforts, the three men listened. Ben heard nothing, and Patrick wasn't sure, but Joe, with his younger ears, could hear something. The wind? He doubted it. A groan, maybe. Could be a wild critter, he thought, but then he heard a definite sound. One which both Ben and Patrick heard, too.

The snort of a horse, then the tapping of metal on rock.

Instantly, the three dismounted and drew their weapons. Whatever or whoever was making that noise might not be friendly.

Leaving their horses parked where they were, the three split up to make a more difficult target. Joe to the left, Ben in the centre and Patrick on the right. They started to walk forwards, almost on tiptoe to keep the noise low.

All sorts of sounds kept assailing Joe's ears: scampering, fluttering, sighs and groans seemed to come from all around in a gentle cacophony.

Then, just as the jitters began to take over, Joe saw a pair of red eyes almost straight in front of him.

'Jesus!' Joe yelled and dived to the ground, Ben and Patrick followed suit.

A burbling groan came from ahead, and the three men swallowed – heavily.

TWELVE

By ten o'clock that night, there were five men who hadn't reported back to Blarney Farm: Joe, Ben and Patrick, as well as the two cowboys who'd camped out in the desert for the night.

Doug Cartwright and Pat had been the last to return, their crestfallen faces adding to the assembled group.

Pat, in the absence of his father, took control. 'There ain't a whole lot we can do tonight,' he said stating the obvious. 'But we'll resume in the morning. Did anyone cover their entire area?'

No one answered yes.

'Well, start off where you finished. Sun-up'll be around four-thirty, so let's get some chow an' sleep.' The men started to make their way back to the bunkhouse, Blarney Farm hands and Broken Saddle men together.

'An' by the way,' Pat called after them. 'Thanks for your efforts.'

Martha was still caring for Siobhan as Doug and Pat entered the front parlour.

'Sit awhile with your mother,' Martha said to

Pat. 'I'll get us all some supper, then you two get some sleep.'

Martha walked through to the back kitchen and soon the smell of food being cooked filled the house. Pat sat by his mother, who hadn't moved a muscle – except for her twisting fingers – since the two men had left earlier.

'It's gonna be all right, ma,' Pat said consolingly, but his mother either didn't hear or didn't believe him. She didn't even blink, still staring into the flames that danced in the fireplace.

'She ain't in the cornfield,' Doug said.

'Seems that way. I guess the horse made its way there for the water,' Pat replied.

'Still, we'd better start there first light. See what we can find.'

Martha entered the room. She carried three bowls of stew on a tray. 'Get this down and I'll bring some bread and the coffee pot through,' she said and, without waiting for a reply, left the parlour.

'Ma,' Pat said. 'Here's some stew. You gotta eat, else when Eileen comes home you won't have the strength to tan her hide.'

Although his mother made no physical move, her eyes shifted from the flames to the steaming bowl of stew that her son was holding in front of her. She slowly untwined her fingers and took the bowl in both hands. Pat smiled at her and silently, Siobhan began to eat.

'What the hell's keepin' Pa?' Pat said to Doug, concern filling his mind.

Doug somehow seemed to be a different person to the man Pat had grown up knowing. He had a new-found confidence that seemed to emanate from within.

'Knowin' your pa,' Doug said, 'he ain't likely to give up the search on account of the night.'

'Yeah, you're right. I jus' hope he's okay, that's all.'

*   *   *

The pangs of hunger were now beginning to make themselves felt. Despite the pain from her wrists and ankles and the fetid air she was forced to breathe, Eileen's stomach rumbled.

She had no idea how long she'd been in this cold, dank place. She hadn't heard anything for a long while and she didn't know whether to be pleased about that or not.

Had they just abandoned her here? Left her to die of starvation? Her imagination ran riot at that thought, and her stomach rumbled louder. Then she heard a noise that filled her with dread. A small squeak and a scuffling sound.

The scratching sound magnified until she felt she was surrounded by small animals of the night, because for Eileen, she'd been in the night since she was attacked.

Oh, God! She thought, rats!

On the very edge of panic, Eileen began to move her legs backwards and forwards in the hope of frightening the rats enough to keep them away from her. If her wrists *were* bleeding, then the smell of blood would be more than the rats could ignore.

The ropes round her ankles began to dig into her flesh, but she felt no pain. In fact, she suddenly realized, she couldn't feel her feet at all.

A moan escaped her lips and she began to sob, her chest moving up and down almost in time with her legs. And all the while, the scuffling sounds grew all around her.

*　*　*

'It's a Goddamned horse!' Ben said, getting back to his feet and brushing the sand off his clothes.

Joe and Patrick regained their feet, Joe feeling a little sheepish at panicking so easily.

'Must've been the sunset reflecting off his eyes,' Joe blurted out.

'Ah, well, better to be safe than sorry,' Patrick piped up, and Joe felt a slight sense of relief as Patrick came to his aid.

Patrick walked across to the mare and stroked its head. 'This is my foreman's horse,' he said quietly. 'It belongs to Martin O'Flynn!'

'What the hell's goin' on around here?' Ben almost shouted out. 'Folks're going missing by the minute.'

A soft moan wafted through the air, and instantly, the three were on guard again.

'Who's there?' Ben called out.

He was answered with another groan.

Warily, Ben moved towards the sound. He almost stumbled on the body of Martin O'Flynn.

'Patrick, it's Martin.'

Patrick reholstered his sideiron and knelt by the prone body of his friend and foreman.

'Martin, Martin, can you hear me?' Patrick's voice quivered with emotion.

Martin O'Flynn seemed to drift in and out of consciousness. His eyes opened and he stared blankly at Patrick. His mouth opened and closed but no words came out.

'I can't hear you Martin,' Patrick said and knelt down lower, his ear practically touching O'Flynn's mouth.

Patrick Malloy stood up. In even the near blackness, Ben and Joe could see the anger that rolled across his face in waves.

'What did he say?' Ben asked.

'After all these years,' Patrick said. 'After all this time, they still come back to haunt me.'

'Who?' Ben shouted. 'Who?'

'My worst nightmare, that's who,' Patrick said. 'I don't know for certain, but I've got a bad feeling, a real bad feeling.'

'What the devil you talkin' about?' Ben was almost beside himself with frustration.

'I hired three hands last week. Three cowboys to ride fence for a few days. Stacey, Palmer and Young.'

'So?' Joe said.

'You're too young to remember, boy,' Patrick said. 'But your daddy knows. You do, don't you

Ben?' Patrick stared into the deep brown eyes of his friend.

'It can't be the same men,' Ben said. 'Not after all this time.'

'Maybe it isn't. But in my heart of hearts, I've always lived in fear of them returning, so I have.'

Joe began to catch on to their conversation. He may have been young, but he had a good memory.

'First thing we gotta do,' Joe said, 'is get Martin back to Blarney Farm.'

This seemed to shake the two men. 'You're right, of course we must,' Patrick said.

He knelt again and began to feel Martin's body. His hand came up wet and sticky.

'I'll light a fire,' Joe said. He felt better doing something.

'We'll have you as right as rain in no time,' Patrick said.

Unseen by any of them, O'Flynn grinned.

*   *   *

Parking their animals to the rear of the cabin, the three badmen entered the single, bare room and flopped down on the wooden floorboards.

'Better check on the girl,' Palmer said. 'Make sure she ain't dead nor nothin'.' He grinned maliciously.

Harley Young walked across the floor to the trapdoor and lifted it.

'It's as black as hell down there,' he said.

'Ain't much better up here,' Stacey replied.

Harley grunted and they heard his footsteps as he descended the steps.

'You dead?' they heard him ask.

'Dumb sonuvabitch!' Palmer said, more to himself than anyone else.

They heard a dull thud as Harley none too gently kicked Eileen's thigh. Then a high pitched scream.

'Fer Christ's sake, Harley,' Palmer shouted, 'gag that bitch!'

'She's wearing that sack,' Harley replied.

'Well take the damn thing off then, and gag her!'

'But she'll see me,' Harley said.

'Harley, you cain't see your hand in front o' your face, how's she gonna see you?'

Harley didn't reply.

To Eileen, the removal of the sack was like a breath of fresh air. She couldn't see the face of the man who was roughly tying a sweat-filled bandanna round her mouth, but she breathed in deeply through her nose.

Even though the air in the cellar was dank and musty, it was a damn sight better than the smell the sacking had carried with it. She only hoped and prayed that he didn't put it back on.

Harley finished tying the bandanna and had other thoughts on his mind. It had been a long time since he'd been with a woman and the smell of Eileen was driving him fit to bust.

Making sure the gag was good and tight, he knelt down beside her, his face only inches from her. He smelled her hair, and then ran his grimy fingers through it. It felt different. Long and soft.

His hand fell to her shoulder and he felt the girl flinch.

Harley chuckled.

'Now come on, girl,' he whispered. 'There ain't nothin' to be scairt for, I'm jus' making sure you's all right.'

His hand slid down her chest and stopped when it reached the gentle mound of her left breast.

Eileen squirmed. She could smell the filth on the man and his hand burned through her clothes and filled her with disgust.

'Ain't no sense in you a-wrigglin', little lady,' Harley said.

Eileen squealed.

'Ain't nobody gonna hear you,' Harley said and he roughly grabbed her other breast as well, squeezing hard.

Despite herself, Eileen could feel her nipples growing hard as Harley rubbed and rubbed and rubbed.

Suddenly, a blindingly bright light hit her eyes. Eileen could see nothing. The only thing she noticed was that the hands left her body.

'You bastard!' she heard a voice say.

'I was only feelin' her,' another voice said.

There was a thump.

'Git back up those stairs!'

Dan Stacey had heard the noises from below and, lighting an old newspaper, he'd come down to investigate. He, too, couldn't remember the last time he'd been with a woman, but there was a thread of decency in him that wouldn't allow Harley to rape her.

'Sorry, ma'am,' was all he said and Eileen, through her closed eyelids, saw the bright light diminish as Stacey left the cellar.

All the time Eileen had been in the cellar, it was only her life she'd been worried about; now, there was maybe something else these men wanted.

Her wild thoughts were stifled by a roar of laughter coming from above and a loud voice.

'Hell, we might as well have some fun with her afore we kill her!'

THIRTEEN

Martin O'Flynn's wounds were worse than they'd at first thought.

Joe had built a campfire which doubled as heat, but more importantly, light, so they could see what they were up against.

The slug had entered O'Flynn's chest high up on the left below the shoulder. Broken bone showed through the gaping hole and, on inspection, Ben could see the slug hadn't come out the rear.

'It's still in there,' Ben said to Patrick, 'an' it'll take more expertise than I have to get it out.'

'How you feeling, Martin?' Patrick asked.

O'Flynn coughed in reply, his face screwing up in obvious pain.

'Do you think you can ride?' Patrick asked the stricken man.

Again, O'Flynn coughed, but this time he forced out an answer. 'I sure as hell don't want to finish off me days out here.' He smiled weakly up at Patrick.

'Best we can do,' Patrick went on, 'is to patch you up as much as we can and then get back to

Broken Saddle as fast as we can.'

O'Flynn coughed again and a thin trickle of blood ran from his lips and down his stubbly chin. He nodded his agreement.

'Come on,' Ben said, 'let's get started.'

Using their shirts for bandages, they bound up Martin's chest as tightly as they could. The bleeding was down to a trickle, but it hadn't stopped. Ben only hoped they could get him back before he drowned in his own blood.

With Patrick on one side and Ben on the other, they got Martin painfully to his feet. Joe brought his horse across and lifted Martin's left leg into the stirrup, then all three men hoisted him aboard.

Martin barely had the strength to swing his right leg across the saddle, but Joe took care of that, making sure his boot was firmly placed in the other stirrup.

'I'm gonna tie you to the horse, Martin,' Patrick said. 'We don't want you making a nose-dive to the dirt every five minutes.'

Using his lariat and the stirrup straps to secure him, Patrick, as gentle as he could but knowing the ropes must be secure, fastened Martin to the saddle.

Joe held onto the horse while Ben and Patrick mounted up, then he handed them the reins before mounting up himself.

With Martin's horse between them, the quartet set off back to Broken Saddle. O'Flynn groaned and grunted for a while, but eventually, either through loss of blood, the shock to his system or pain, he lost consciousness. Ben, Joe and Patrick were at least thankful for that.

*   *   *

Young Pat Malloy was getting restless. The fact that neither Ben, Joe or his father had returned was playing on his mind too much to sleep.

He decided he'd head out to Broken Saddle. just in case they'd decided to go there first.

Doug Cartwright wouldn't let him go alone, he even insisted on getting a half dozen men to ride with them.

Martha, too, was concerned about her husband. Awake in an overstuffed armchair, she heard the voices and the pacing of Doug and Pat. Getting up from the chair, she went to the back kitchen, to find the two men.

'With all this talking and walking up and down, it makes it impossible for a body to get any sleep,' she said half scoldingly.

'We're going to Broken Saddle,' Pat said without preamble. 'Just in case they went back there.'

'And I'm coming with you,' Martha said.

'I think it best you stay with my mother,' Pat said.

'Oh, there's enough folk with your mother,' Martha countered. 'She'll be fine. We're only an hour away, so I daresay we can send a rider with any news.'

Pat saw the same look in Martha Dowie's eyes

that he'd seen so often in his own mother's. The look that said 'My mind's made up and there's nothing you can do or say that will change it!'

Pat capitulated. 'Okay, let's go.'

The buggy was hitched up and, along with six hands, they set off for Broken Saddle. Doug Cartwright had issued orders to the remaining men, so the search would continue unabated come sun-up.

It took them just over an hour and a half to reach the ranch-house. What hands were left there earlier were abed and there were no lights showing in the house.

'I guess they didn't come back here, then,' Pat said, disappointment showing in his voice.

'Not yet,' Martha said, 'but that doesn't mean to say they won't be. Come on, let's get the fire lit and coffee on ready for when they do.'

Leaving the buggy hitched outside, they entered the ranch-house and set to lighting all the oil lamps they could muster, Pat lit the big wood burner in the kitchen and Doug set a fire going in the parlour.

Then, with guards posted outside, they sat down to drink coffee to keep themselves awake. And they waited.

* * *

The long journey back to Broken Saddle proved uneventful. Martin O'Flynn had an inner strength that, despite the pain and discomfort he felt, kept him alive.

Coming down the trail from the north, they hit

the wooden entrance to the ranch and, as ever, Ben raised his hand to touch the saddle mounted atop the poles as he passed through. They could see the lights of the ranch-house as they neared and, before they'd got to within a hundred yards, Pat was out to meet them.

'Any news?' he asked.

'If you mean Eileen, no,' his father replied.

Pat then saw Martin O'Flynn: 'Oh, God!' Pat ran to Martin's horse. 'What's happened?'

'We found him along the north fence,' Ben said. 'He'd been trailing those three new men your father hired two days ago.'

'And they did this?' Pat asked.

'Reckon so. Martin regained consciousness and told us their names. He didn't see them shoot him, but he knows they did.'

'Come on,' Patrick intervened. 'Let's get Martin inside. Pat, is Siobhan here?'

'No, she's still at Blarney Farm. We came back here to see if you were here,' Pat replied.

'Right, I'll get home. I'll be back at first light.'

Without waiting for a reply, Patrick Malloy wheeled his animal and set off back to his farm.

'Come on, Pat, give me a hand with Martin.' With Joe helping, the three men untied the ropes and, as gently as they could, they lowered Martin from his horse. He was still unconscious, but the blood that had stained the makeshift bandages hadn't spread too much.

Martha, once over the initial shock, took control. She undressed O'Flynn, bathed the wound and rebandaged him.

'He needs a doctor,' she said to her husband. 'I've done as much as I can do.'

'I'll ride to town,' Pat volunteered. 'I should be back come sun-up.'

'Thanks, Pat. You bring the doc back here. If you're not back by sunrise, we'll be out along the north fence.'

'Okay.' Pat smiled and left to go to town.

'You get to bed, Ben,' Martha said. 'I'll stay with Martin. He's beginning to run a fever, he can't be left alone.'

Ben took his wife into his arms and, although he would rather feel her body curled up alongside his in bed, he had to agree she was right.

'I'll see you at dawn,' he said. 'Wake me if you need help.'

'I will. Now, off you go.'

* * *

'By the time you get there it'll be sun-up,' Palmer said to Harley Young. 'Now git!'

'Supposin' there's gunplay?' Harley moaned.

'I keep a-tellin' ya. There won't *be* no gunplay. All you gotta do, if'n anybody sees you is to tell 'em if anything happens to you, the girl's dead.'

Harley wasn't convinced, but he knew better than to argue with Luke Palmer.

Harley Young saddled up reluctantly. He couldn't see the sense in riding out to Blarney Farm *or* Broken Saddle. As far as he could make out, it was his neck and only his neck that was on the line.

Kidnapping was a capital offence, he'd be hanged for sure.

Luke Palmer watched as Harley rode out of the blind canyon, Stacey was fast asleep next to the trapdoor.

Palmer rubbed his beard-growth. His thoughts were in the cellar and the pretty young thing that was down there all alone.

He felt a heat in his groin as he moved towards the trapdoor.

FOURTEEN

Pat Malloy junior got back with the doc just five minutes' before the sun began to appear over the eastern desert.

Already, the men were up and about – washing, getting coffee and breakfast – all eager to get on with the hunt.

Anticipation was high that morning. They now had a pretty good idea of the perpetrators.

Saddling up, the men formed a small group round the front steps of the ranch-house.

It was Ben who saw the lone rider approaching the entrance to the ranch.

Harley Young, his rifle gripped in his left hand, rode slowly towards the broken saddle perched on top of the entranceway. He could see the knot of men in front of the house and his natural reaction was to rein in, wheel about and ride for high leather out of there.

He knew that would be useless. If the cowpokes didn't catch him, then Luke Palmer would kill him for sure. Harley had no choice. Taking a deep breath and swallowing harder than he thought possible with a throat drier than a bleached steer skeleton, he rode towards the entrance.

Ben mounted up and rode as slowly to the only way into the compound, he was followed by Pat and two other hands.

Ben dismounted and waited for the rider to arrive. It was Pat who recognized the incoming cowboy. He instantly drew his sideiron.

'Mr Dowie, it's Harley Young, he's one the three men that …'

'Hold on there, Pat,' Ben said, 'let's see what he wants, afore we start to shootin'.'

'Got a message fer yuh,' Harley shouted from what he hoped to be a safe distance.

'Bring it on in,' Ben called back.

'I'd jus' as soon leave it here, mister,' Harley shouted out.

'Show him your guns, boys,' Ben said.

The three men behind him drew their weapons.

'Now, bring it on in,' Ben said. 'Nice an' easy.'

Harley sat atop his horse for a few seconds before deciding he had no choice. Digging his spurs in, he urged the animal forward at a walking pace. When he was no more than thirty feet from the fence line, Ben called a halt.

'Hold it right there, mister. Now, get down.'

Harley did as he was ordered without even thinking. His rifle was still gripped tight in his left hand. The red shirt he wore, stained and dust-filled was now black under his armpits and down his back as the sweat began to pour out of his body.

Harley walked forward, in his left hand the rifle, in his right, the note that Luke Palmer had written.

Without saying a word, Harley handed the note to Ben. With three guns trained on the intruder, Ben had no qualms in taking the piece of paper.

He read it, and his face turned to thunder. 'Where is she?' he spat.

'If 'n you start anythin',' Harley almost wailed, 'you'll never see her alive.'

Ben took two steps forwards and without warning swung a huge fist which connected with Harley's chin, sending the man flying backwards.

'I asked you a question, boy!' Ben said.

'I ain't sayin' nuthin',' Harley replied, tears in his eyes and an ache in his jaw that told him it was maybe broken.

Ben drew his Colt and pointed it at the head of the prone Harley, who was by now leaning on one elbow rubbing his chin.

'You got five seconds, mister,' Ben said.

Harley stared up at the man. He didn't recognize him from all those years ago, he hadn't had a good look at any of them. A thousand thoughts fluttered through Harley's brain. The main one was that Palmer had been wrong about the gunplay. The look in the man's eyes told him that he wasn't bluffing. Harley had seen that look before – many times – in the eyes of Luke Palmer.

'One,' Ben began.

'It ain't no use, mister,' Harley pleaded. 'Palmer'll kill her as sure as sure.'

'Two.'

'I'm tellin' you, mister.'

'Three.'

'It's more'n my life's worth, mister.' Harley was almost sobbing now.

'Four.' Ben Dowie cocked the hammer of his Colt.

'It ain't my fault, mister,' Harley cried. 'It weren't my idea. I didn't want to track you folks down, even though it was my big brother you killed back there in the desert.'

Ben could hardly believe what he was hearing. After all these years, these bandits had come for them again!

His thoughts were interrupted as Patrick Malloy rode down the trail heading for Broken Saddle. He saw the group of men at the entrance, then saw the man lying in the dirt.

'You filthy scum!' Malloy shouted as he jumped from his horse. He rushed at Harley, his boot connecting with his thigh. Harley wailed in pain.

'Where's my daughter?' Patrick yelled.

Harley was silent. Patrick took his pistol out and held it, cocked.

'I'll not be asking you again,' he said through clenched teeth.

Harley Young closed his eyes. He'd seen his own death approaching.

Patrick squeezed the trigger. The slug landed in the dirt, dust and grit flew up into Harley's face. He could stand it no more.

'All right, all right, she's in a cabin, north of

here. Palmer and Stacey are still there.' Harley hung his head and sobbed.

Patrick Malloy cocked his handgun again.

'Wait, Patrick,' Ben rushed to his friend's side. 'Let the law take care of him. You pull the trigger an' it'll make you no better than them.'

Patrick stood rock still; anger and hatred filled his eyes, but what Ben said was true.

'Get him out of my sight,' he said eventually.

The two cowpokes replaced their unused weapons and, grabbing their lariats, they tied Harley up and frog-marched him to the bunkhouse.

'We got work to do,' Patrick said and mounted up. Joe and Pat arrived at the scene just as Ben and Patrick were heading off.

'Get the boys,' Ben called back over his shoulder. 'Eileen's in the old cabin in Half Moon Canyon.'

Pat turned his horse and rode back to the ranch-house. Joe kept on riding.

It took the three men less that forty-minutes' hard gallop to reach the mouth of the canyon.

They hid their horses and grabbed their rifles and as much ammo as they could carry. Patrick walked forward, sticking to the rocky sides of the canyon until the cabin came into view. It looked deserted.

Pointing, he motioned for Ben to take the other side of the canyon and with Joe in the centre, keeping low, the three men crept forward.

* * *

Luke Palmer never made it to the trapdoor. Just as he was about to try and lift it, Stacey woke up, his gun sprang into his hand as if by magic.

'What's goin' on?' he stammered in a still-asleep voice.

'Jus' checkin' on the girl,' Palmer said, licking his lips. Although quick himself, Palmer knew that Stacey was quicker and he didn't want to risk a gunfight.

'I reckon she'll be okay,' Stacey said, wide awake now.

Palmer backed off, but the look in his eyes was pure hatred fuelled by madness. Stacey knew he'd have to keep a close eye on his 'partner'.

Palmer stood, stretched and walked across the creaking floorboards towards the door. He walked with the gait of a man sure of himself and Stacey never took his eyes off his right hand for a second.

Opening the door, Palmer breathed in deeply. 'Think I'll take me a piss,' he said.

Stacey stood up, his gun still in his right hand. He watched as Palmer walked through the door.

A single shot rang out and Palmer flew back inside the cabin.

Stacey wasn't sure at first whether Palmer was shooting at him or not and so as the big man crashed back inside, Stacey let off two quick shots.

Palmer's body twitched a couple of times, then didn't move again. It was then that Stacey saw that Palmer's gun was still holstered. He froze.

The shots echoed round the blind canyon and gradually filtered out to the desert where the two cowboys had resumed their tracking. They reached the canyon mouth atop their horses and saw first Patrick and then Ben. Joe was lying low in the centre of the trail using the small rise in the trail for cover.

The two dismounted in full view of the cabin. before Patrick or Ben could motion to them, two rifle shots rang out and the cowboys crumpled to the floor.

Neither man was dead. One got winged, and he crawled over to his partner who got gut-shot. The man was in agony, his legs kicking and twitching as both hands held on to his guts.

His partner, getting to his knees, grabbed him under the arms and began to slow drag him out of the line of fire.

'I'm okay, jus' winged,' he yelled to the two men he'd seen. 'I'm getting him clear.'

'Stay low,' Ben called back.

A steady stream of bullets came from the cabin. The man inside was taking his time, aiming each shot carefully. He had the advantage, even though outnumbered, as he had the girl.

Moving backwards, Stacey shooting through the window, reached down with his right hand and pulled the trapdoor open. He moved back to the window again and loosed off a few more shots to keep the men outside low long enough for him to bring the girl up.

He knew that the only way out of this situation

was to use her as as a shield.

Satisfied he'd bought himself enough time to get down the cellar steps, Stacey rested his rifle against the wall and all but jumped clear onto the cellar floor.

Eileen, terror filling her eyes as she thought her time was nigh, stared through the blackness as the shape approached.

'Now don't you fret none,' Stacey said as he untied the ropes from round her ankles. 'I ain't fixin' to harm you none.' He then removed the rope from the floor post but quickly retied it round her numb wrists.

'No sudden moves,' Stacey said. 'Come on, up the steps.'

With Eileen in front of him, Stacey forced the girl forwards. Eileen's legs were like jelly; fear and being tied up for so long had taken their toll on her muscles. Stacey almost lifted her up the steps.

He picked up his rifle, keeping one arm round Eileen's neck. His smell, sweat, fear and dirt, filled her nostrils and the closeness of his filthy body almost made her sick.

'I'm comin' out,' yelled Stacey so close to Eileen's ear that it rang with the noise. 'An' you better hold your fire,' Stacey shouted out again. 'I got me a shield.'

Pushing Eileen forward again, he reached the door. Palmer's left leg blocked the door swinging open, and Stacey lashed out viciously with his boot, almost turning Palmer's body over in the process.

He pulled the door wide open and stood framed

there while he tried to see his attackers and make sure they saw the girl.

'Now, throw out your weapons,' Stacey called. 'I ain't jokin'.'

Ben, Joe and Patrick could see the riding gown that Eileen was wearing, but they couldn't see her face.

'Step outside,' Ben called. 'We want to see Eileen first.'

Stacey pushed Eileen forward so that they both now stood outside the cabin.

'You see her?' Stacey called out.

They all did. So the man wasn't bluffing.

Patrick stood up, both arms in the air. He threw the rifle he'd been holding to the ground.

Ben saw him and followed suit. Patrick was Eileen's father and he called the tune.

Joe stayed low.

Stacey pushed Eileen down the single step. 'Now, I'm goin' fer my horse,' Stacey said, 'an' we are ridin' out o' here, nice and easy. Got it?'

'Yeah, we hear you,' Patrick replied, his hands still up.

'Both of you, start walkin' towards the cabin. When I'm mounted up, the girl'll be in front of me all the way an' my pistol'll be right up against her head. Un'erstand?'

'Yeah, we understand.' Patrick began to walk towards the cabin and Ben followed. Joe remained hidden, sweat pouring from him in a torrent. He didn't know if it was fear, excitement, or the danger Eileen was in that had made him stay low.

He just needed one good, clear shot.

Stacey reached his horse. Harley hadn't bothered to unsaddle them, and for once, Stacey was grateful for that. He climbed into the saddle, keeping a tight hold on the ropes that bound Eileen's arms behind her back, and then roughly hauled her into the saddle in front of him.

Jolting the reins, he urged the animal ahead.

Ben and Patrick, no more than twenty feet away from the cabin, watched as the horse and its two riders appeared from the rear of the cabin.

Patrick's face melted as he saw his daughter: her face ashen, dirty and fear in her eyes, it was all he could do to stop himself rushing the madman that held her.

'Steady, Patrick,' Ben whispered. 'Steady.'

A smirk appeared on Stacey's face when he saw the two men. He recognized Ben, even after all this time, and, for some strange reason, Ben recognized him.

'Long time, old man,' Stacey said.

'Not long enough,' Ben spat back.

'Inside!' Stacey ordered.

They both walked towards the door of the cabin, neither man taking their eyes off Stacey.

They reached the step and stopped. Stacey moved the horse forwards and began edging out of the canyon. He was close enough to the two men to see their empty holsters. 'Inside!' he ordered again.

Reluctantly, Ben and Patrick stepped into the dark cabin. On the floor was the body of the third man and beside him – a rifle!

'Close the door!' Stacey yelled and Ben did as he was told.

As soon as the door swung to, Stacey kicked his spurs into his animal's flanks and headed for the open range.

It was just what Doug Cartwright was hoping for.

He'd been with Martha and the doc while they were attending Martin O'Flynn, and by the time he'd come outside, it was just in time to see Patrick, Ben and Joe disappearing into the distance.

Getting the story from the two cowboys escorting Harley Young to the bunkhouse, Doug made up his mind on his intent.

He set off in pursuit, but detoured north-east and climbed the rock face at the rear of Half Moon Canyon.

Now, perched high above the canyon, his rifle trained on the rider as he began to leave, Doug steadied his hands, took a deep breath and, with little difficulty, recaptured the image of his dead wife's face in his mental eye.

Sighting down the blued-barrel of his Winchester, Doug Cartwright gently squeezed the trigger, feeling metal slide through oil on metal as the trigger came back towards him. He felt the slight resistance as the hammer engaged, heard the small click prior to the explosive force of the shell as it sent the slug shooting out of the barrel.

Too late, Dan Stacey heard the shot echoing

down the canyon. With Eileen in front of him, Stacey had nowhere to turn.

The slug shattered his spine and punctured both lungs as the lead slug spun through his body. The force slumped him forward, squashing Eileen's chest up against the neck of the horse.

She fell forward, hands still tied behind her back, and Stacey landed beside her. Dead.

Joe was first on the scene, fearing that Eileen had been hit and he searched her clothing, frantic with worry, looking for blood.

Relief flooded his face when he found nothing. He untied the ropes and lifted her head, resting it in the crook of his arms. He hugged her tightly.

Doug Cartwright stood and waved down into the canyon as Ben and Patrick ran from the cabin towards Joe and Eileen.

'Yee-howw!' the sound echoed round the small canyon and Doug Cartwright's face beamed.

Eileen opened her eyes. The bright sunlight was too much for her and it took a while for her to be able to focus on Joe's face.

'In Ireland,' she began, 'they have a custom that whenever there's a leap year, a lady can propose.' She smiled up into Joe's face.

'If that's your proposal,' Joe said, 'this is my acceptance.' He leant down and they kissed.

'Seems like there's no need for us to hang around here,' Patrick said to Ben.

'Think not?' Ben said and laughed.

'I most certainly think not,' Patrick said and the two men slowly rode back to Broken Saddle.

R